Tears, Fears, and Fame

Laura Thomas

For Alex ~

Blessings & joy!

♡ I hope you enjoy this book
Alex... I'm a singer, too!
God bless you ~ feel free
to contact me anytime
through my website ...
www.laurathomas
author.com
X

Publishers Note:
This is a work of fiction. All names, characters, places, and events are the work of the author's imagination. Any resemblance to real persons, places, or events is coincidental.

Copyright ©Laura Thomas 2015
All rights reserved
ISBN 13: 9780692596692
ISBN 10:0692596690

D W B   P U B L I S H I N G
www.dancingwithbearpublishing.com

Dedicated to my three sisters...

~ *One* ~

Sara held her breath and read the latest message on the screen. It was from him again, she knew without even checking. Of course, he used a different email account each time but he always signed off the same way. Maybe the message wasn't threatening enough to alert the authorities, but it certainly caused her pulse to quicken. She squeezed her eyes shut and slammed the laptop lid.

When the messages first started to appear, Sara thought it might be a joke—possibly even someone trying to make her feel important. Fame was way out of her comfort zone, and so far, she managed to avoid a full-on panic attack but this could be her undoing. She couldn't bear to surrender her dream, yet right now, a normal, quiet, boring life sounded like paradise. Tonight's message crossed a line. Sara bit her lip until she tasted blood.

"There you are." Natasha sauntered into the room, tossed her phone upon the coffee table, and sank onto the sofa next to her friend. "I can't believe I'm actually at home on a Friday evening. What has become of my life?"

Sara attempted to slow down her erratic breathing. She was on the verge of a meltdown.

"What's wrong?" Natasha swiveled and stared at Sara. "You look totally stressed and distraught. The fantastic life of fame getting too much for you?"

That was the final straw—Sara dissolved into tears.

Natasha's face crumpled. "Hey, I'm sorry, girl. I was only joking. Whatever is the matter? I'm usually the crazy one riding the emotional roller coaster around here. You're the sensible, levelheaded one. Remember?"

Natasha moved closer to Sara, and hugged her along with the laptop. "Now, now, it can't be all that bad. Let's see, you're acing every subject in eleventh grade, you're the freshest face and newest recording artist for Gracelight Agency. Plus, you get to live with me for a while, which is beyond amazing. I know I'm not much good at compassion but I can't imagine what's got you so rattled. Can you tell me?"

Sara placed her laptop on the coffee table and wiped her face on her sleeve. She took several slow, deep breaths and eventually, the sobbing subsided.

"I'm sorry, Natasha. I know I'm being silly. I have so much to be grateful for and I'm truly happy. I love everything about my life right now. Your parents are so kind to let me stay here with you while I finish high school. I still can't believe I get to live in such luxury at the same time as pursuing my singing career. It's like I'm living some bizarre fairy tale."

Natasha shrugged and gazed around the spacious living room, which looked like it belonged in a home design magazine. "It's only stuff. Even my parents are starting to see how superficial it is now. They were thrilled to help you out, and quite honestly, you bring some life into this boring mansion. I'm getting used to having you around. Who'd have ever thought we would be such friends?"

Sara attempted a smile. "I know I was your little project in the beginning but I think we're past that now."

"Was I that obvious?" Natasha sighed. "I guess I came across as a wretched princess and a spoiled brat at first. I think I've changed though, don't you?"

Sara looked into the genuine eyes of the beautiful girl who once upon a time wanted nothing to do with her. "Absolutely, Natasha. That mission's trip experience in Mexico was life changing for you. I'm blessed to be up close to see it all. I honestly can't imagine your parents apart now. They seem so in love."

Natasha scrunched her nose. "Yeah, it's kind of gross but kind of marvelous. We experienced our fair share of miracles this year, that's for sure. I'm grateful it didn't all end in divorce. But don't change the subject, what's up with you tonight? What are the tears for? Are you going to tell me, or do I have to phone Beth and ask her to come and help with the interrogation?"

"No, please don't bother Bethany. I know she's going to the movies with some of the Youth Group, and I don't want to ruin her plans."

Natasha huffed. "By 'some of the Youth Group' I presume you mean Todd. Considering they are still not officially dating, they're doing a pretty good impersonation of a dating couple."

"Oh, be nice. I know there are at least five of them hanging out together tonight."

"Whatever. Okay then, it's just you and me. Spill."

Sara stood and wandered over to the massive picture window, which overlooked the meticulous grounds and kidney-shaped swimming pool. She shivered at the sight of the deepening wintry sky, and tugged her sweater sleeves down over her hands. "Do you ever worry about security? I mean, living in this posh neighborhood and everything?"

Natasha snorted. "Are you kidding me? Daddy has the top security system installed, and so do all the other houses in this cul-de-sac." She joined Sara at the window. "Why? Have you seen someone suspicious or creepy?"

"No, nothing like that. I'm sorry—I don't want to freak you out. It's just that I've received some weird emails and stuff lately."

"No way. Are you kidding me? Why didn't you tell me before? I saw a crazy documentary on cyber-bullying last week. I realize the whole notion of me and a documentary is absurd but I couldn't stop watching it." She took Sara's hand and pulled her back to the sofa. "Tell me everything."

Sara nibbled her fingernail for a moment, and then took a deep breath. "Okay, it started right after I got the recording contract with Gracelight."

"What? That's months ago."

"I know. I should have told someone. At first, I didn't pay much attention to the messages. It was more annoying than threatening, that's why I kept quiet. As soon as my name was in the local paper and a couple of magazines, there were a few random strangers who wanted to be my friend on social media, and followed my posts a bit too enthusiastically. Everyone warned me it could happen, so I tried not to let it bug me.

Personally, I'd rather keep a really low profile and lead a quiet life, but my agent wants me to be more public, and I understand. It's good for publicity and promotion."

Natasha's face grew pale. "I hope this isn't my fault. After all, it was my big mouth that started all this fame in the first place. I couldn't help it. You've got serious talent, and I knew Mother had contacts she could connect with..."

"Oh no. I'm not blaming you at all. I'm absolutely thrilled to be in the Christian music industry. It's my dream come true. I'll always be thankful to you for sending off my CD, even if I was the last one to know about it." She grinned and squeezed Natasha's hands. "I knew it was going to be a challenge for me. I'm super shy and klutzy, and would rather curl up with a good book than perform in a concert, but I'm getting used to it."

Natasha reached for the laptop. "So what's all this about then? Is it really a cyber-stalker, like on that TV documentary? It's a coward's game, you know. Bullying and harassing from a safe distance, knowing there's little chance of them ever getting caught. And it could be a little old lady or a pimply teen boy, or anyone in between. "

Sara cringed. "At least it's only on the Internet, so I guess he's harmless enough."

"He?"

"Yeah. He calls himself *The Eagle*." Her mouth went dry.

"*The Eagle*? He has a name?"

Tears blurred Sara's vision when she tried to focus on the screen before her. "He says I'm nothing but a quiet little mouse who sings." She shrugged. "I get it. I am kind of mousey in a way. I tried not to let the words bother me. You know, 'sticks and stones may break my bones, but names will never hurt me'."

"That's insane. Who does that? And there is nothing mousey about you, Sara Dean." Natasha's eyes flashed. "This *Eagle* better hope he never runs into me, that's all I can say. I'll give him a piece of my mind." She nudged Sara's hand on the laptop. "But if it's been going on for months, how come you're so skittish tonight?"

"See for yourself. Read today's message."

Natasha squinted at the screen. "Where? Oh, here we are." She read the sentence out loud.

"'*You can PRAY as much as you want,*
little mouse. But remember you are
MY PREY. The Eagle.'"

Natasha's mouth dropped open, and she shuddered. "Oh my word, that is totally not cool. He could be some crazy who actually wants to hurt you. I don't know why you've been bottling this up on your own, Sara, but seriously, this needs to end now before *The Eagle* decides to pay you a visit in person."

11

~ *Two* ~

"*B*eth, it's Natasha. I'm glad I caught you. I don't want to explain over the phone, but you need to get over here stat. We have an issue to sort out with Sara. Yes, fine. Ciao."

Sara padded into the living room carrying two glasses of water and handed one to Natasha. "Oh no, you didn't interrupt Bethany's night, did you? There's no need."

"Yes, there most certainly is. This is serious. Besides, she spends way too much time with Todd for my liking. And I'm not jealous, before you even think it. You're lucky I didn't phone Alice as well. In fact, Beth's aunt is next on my list."

Sara shook her head. "I knew this would happen. I shouldn't have said anything. I realize you mean well, but I hate to cause a fuss. Maybe I should call my parents and move back home..."

"Really?" Natasha stood with her hands on her hips and a smirk on her face. "You want to tell them you have a stalker, when they're giving you such a hard time about your singing contract with Gracelight? It's not like they actually care, except maybe for the money you send them."

"That's not fair." Sara jutted her chin. "They do care, they're busy with my little brothers, that's all. James is really moody lately, and they're worried about him hanging with some older kids in the neighborhood. It's not a neighborhood like yours, Natasha—think the complete opposite. They can't help it if they're not rich. Life has always been a struggle."

Natasha sighed and curled up on the sofa. "Sorry, you're right. I still have issues with my big mouth, in case you haven't noticed."

"You're definitely improving."

"I must have been horrific." Natasha shuddered. "But I still don't think it's a good idea to worry them. Not yet at least. It might be something we can figure out before it gets to be a big deal. Besides, Alice is more like a mother to you, and she'll know exactly what to do."

Sara swiped at her long curls. She hated to involve Bethany's Aunt Alice, especially when she was busy planning her upcoming wedding, but Natasha was right. Alice was there for her at every turn offering encouragement, a listening ear, and whatever else was needed. Not only had she taken on legal guardianship of her niece when Bethany's parents were killed in a car crash, she was a mentor, friend, and pseudo-mother to both Natasha and Sara with their differing needs.

"Alright." Sara sighed dramatically. "I know Alice and Steve will know what to do, but let's not ruin their Friday evening as well, okay? I'll call her in the morning."

"Deal. Unless Beth thinks we should involve them tonight." Natasha set her glass on the table and flitted toward the foyer. "I'm going upstairs to see if my parents left yet. They had some big fundraiser dinner thing to go to. I don't want them eavesdropping or getting suspicious. Mother will worry all night and then it'll be my fault their fundraiser is a flop. I'll be right back."

"I suppose we should explain the situation to them in the morning, too." Sara bit her lip. "I'm probably overreacting. It's most likely nothing. I'm glad *The Eagle* hasn't mentioned me living here, but the last thing I want to do is be a burden. Your dad will probably suggest I move back home. Maybe I should start packing—"

"Whoa." Natasha rushed back to Sara and took hold of both of her shoulders. "Slow down there. Daddy loves you like a daughter. In fact, I think he secretly prefers you to me. Secondly, my mother wouldn't hear of you moving out. You know she's proud of you and wants to keep a close

13

eye on your singing career, seeing as how she was pretty instrumental in it. Thirdly, I don't think you are overreacting. I am the one who goes ballistic over menial issues. You never make a fuss about anything, and that tells me this is something deep. We need to figure it out."

"Okay." Sara took a deep breath. "You go ahead and make sure your parents are heading out soon. I'll keep a low profile in here for now. Your mom will notice I've been crying straight away if she sees me."

"Oh, yes. Nothing gets past Mother. I'll tell them Beth's coming over and we're having a girly night."

"Thanks."

Natasha closed the living room door behind her. Sara collapsed on the sofa and buried her head in her hands.

Why is this bothering me so much? I knew it would be tough being in the limelight. God, don't You want me to sing like this? Do You have other plans? I don't want to carry on if it's not what You want for me. And I don't want to put Natasha's family in danger. Or any of my friends, or even my family...

Several minutes passed, and Sara stared at the closed laptop. Why was someone trying to make her life miserable? She strained to hear if Natasha managed to convince her parents that everything was okay. The doorbell chimed, followed by muffled voices coming from the foyer.

Suddenly, the door burst open.

"Hey, what's all this about?" Bethany rushed into the living room with a gust of chilled air and almost suffocated her friend in a tight hug. She settled on the sofa and peeled off her leather jacket. "Natasha didn't give me much of a clue, but I'm worried about you. You're crying— tell me what's wrong."

"Wait for me," Natasha shouted from the front door. "Just waving off the parents. I'll be right there."

Bethany raised one brow, then passed Sara a Kleenex™ from the side table. "I guess we have our orders."

Natasha pirouetted across the room and curled up in an armchair. "Okay, I'm here. I was saying goodbye to the lovebirds. Honestly, I know I was frantic when my parents wanted to divorce, but now they've sorted stuff out, I feel like I'm intruding on a couple of newlyweds. Anyway, go ahead, Sara, and don't leave out any details."

Sara blew a curl from her face. "Okay, but Bethany, I'm sorry we interrupted your evening. It's a fuss about nothing really. I know you were looking forward to seeing that movie, especially as Todd was going, too."

Bethany waved her hand in the air. "Not a problem. Besides, he knows you would never be upset unless there was a good reason. You're the lowest maintenance friend I've ever had." She grinned at Natasha. "No offense."

Natasha flicked Bethany's arm with the end of her toe. "Absolutely none taken."

Sara took a deep breath. "You two are my best friends. We've been through a lot together in the space of two years."

Bethany nodded. "But these past few months have been crazy for you, Sara. Why don't you start from the beginning and tell us what's up."

"Okay. So I guess this whole thing started in Mexico. Up until that mission trip last spring break, I had no idea if I could actually make it in the music industry. I knew I could sing, everyone told me that, but I've always been painfully shy. I simply enjoyed singing at church, and doing school productions."

"And then I came along." Natasha wiggled her eyebrows.

"Exactly. You were knee deep in some heavy issues of your own at that time, but you really encouraged me and got me wondering if I could sing professionally. It had to be in the Christian music industry, I felt strongly about that, and then when we came home and Natasha sent off

15

my homemade CD..."

Bethany cringed. "I still can't believe you didn't even ask Sara's permission about that, Nat."

"Yeah, but it worked, didn't it?" Natasha grinned. "Plus, we have my mother to thank."

"Yes." Sara smiled at the memory. "I'll never forget when your mom handed me that envelope from Gracelight. They met with me the very next week, and before I knew it, my singing career was in motion. It's been a complete whirlwind ever since."

"But a good whirlwind, right?" Bethany squeezed Sara's hand.

"In so many ways, yes." Sara gazed across the room and out at the cold, bleak evening. "If it hadn't happened, I would probably be babysitting right now in my parents' doublewide, trying to make the best of the situation and dreaming of a different future. But here I am, in this gorgeous mansion, worrying about a stalker. It's absurd."

Bethany gasped. "A stalker? What? When did this start?"

Sara reached for her laptop and cradled it in her arms. "Don't worry, it hasn't happened in person. I was so excited when Natasha's father bought me this laptop for my birthday. I never dreamed of having such a nice one of my own. But now I wish I could throw it in the swimming pool and forget everything. Sorry, I know that sounds ungrateful."

"You're being stalked online?" Bethany squinted at the laptop.

"Hopefully it stays online." Natasha grabbed the remote control for the window coverings. "I think we'll feel better discussing this without being in a goldfish bowl."

The blinds whirred on their way down to cover the vast expanse of glass, and the girls sat silently for a moment. The scent from a large vanilla candle filled the room, and Sarah closed her eyes as she listened to the crackling fire.

"What does this person say?" Bethany asked finally. "Are you sure you're not being oversensitive? I'm not being mean, but I know how sweet you are and how easily you could be hurt."

Natasha threw her hands in the air. "Oh, for goodness sake, Beth, the girl is distraught. *The Eagle* is messing with her head."

"The what?"

"*The Eagle.*" Sara shivered. "That's what he calls himself. He says I'm his little mouse. His prey."

"You are not a mouse," Natasha fumed. "If he knew you at all, he would see that you are brave and strong, and have overcome all sorts of fears to follow your dream. There aren't many people your age that can stand on a stage with a microphone in front of hundreds of people, and sing flawlessly and confidently. I know you're out of your element up there, but you are no mouse."

"Not to mention how you juggle your school work, church commitments, providing for your family, and the singing schedule at the studio," Bethany added. "Whatever this jerk is trying to do to you, Sara, you mustn't let him kill your dream."

"I know, I know." Sara smiled at her two greatest fans. "You guys are the best. But I have to admit, he is scaring me now."

"How long has he been bugging you?" Bethany frowned.

"Since the beginning, when I signed with Gracelight."

Natasha threw her hands in the air. "I don't under-stand why you never told us. We're your friends and we could have helped, or at least listened. That's like six months. And you didn't mention it until now?"

"Calm down, Nat." Bethany hugged a fur cushion tightly to her chest. "I think I know why. It's because this girl doesn't have a mean bone in her body, and the last thing in the world she wants to do is cause anyone any stress or pain, including us. Am I right?"

Sara's cheeks heated. "It's probably nothing any-way."

Natasha sat bolt upright in her chair. "Hey, Sara, have you kept all the messages from the creepy one?"

"No. I know it's foolish but I wanted to get rid of them as soon as they popped up. I guess that wasn't the best idea. I only have today's."

"Try not to worry." Bethany leaned over to see the laptop screen. "Approximately how many do you think he's sent?"

Sara sighed. "Twenty-six."

~ *Three* ~

"*T*wenty-six?" Natasha grabbed the phone from the pocket of her skinny jeans. "How on earth have you kept it a secret for so long? That's it. I'm calling Alice and Steve right now."

"Yes, I think we may need to get the police involved, too." Bethany glanced at Sara. "Come here, you're shaking."

Bethany hugged Sara, while Natasha stepped out to the foyer to contact Alice.

Sara sat up and blew her nose. "Please, no police, Bethany. I don't think it's necessary. He's not really a threat. Besides, you know what my parents will do."

Bethany shrugged. "I know they're not exactly thrilled that you live temporarily at Natasha's, or that you have the music contract, but you have to admit—they don't mind the prospect of the money you'll be earning."

Sara sniffled. "If I can help them out, I will. There hasn't been very much yet, but my agent, Megan, is really organized with the money side of things. It could be quite lucrative, and I love the thought of helping my family financially."

"I'll bet Natasha's parents won't accept a dime from you."

"No, the Smithson-Blair family is beyond generous. I think they feel kind of responsible for me. I only hope all this nonsense doesn't upset them."

"Mother and Daddy will be completely fine." Natasha returned to the living room and slid her phone back in her pocket. "We can explain everything tomorrow. They've seen more drama than most, and they're stronger now than they've ever been. We all are." She half-smiled. "Alice and

Steve are on their way over. You'll feel better after we talk with them. I promise."

Sara's shoulders slumped. "You're right, but I hate this."

"It's not your fault some guy is besotted with you." Bethany smiled. "You're a very pretty girl with a voice like an angel."

Sara tugged at her unruly ringlets. "I don't feel very pretty at the moment. My nose must be bright red, and I bet my eyes are all swollen."

"Let's not get started with your eyes." Natasha twirled in front of the fire. "What did that magazine article say? 'Newcomer Sara Dean has the most exquisite eyes, like the turquoise waters of the Caribbean'. You have certainly blossomed, my dear friend. Of course, I can take credit for most of your fabulous new wardrobe, but the eyes are all you."

"Thanks, Natasha." Sara gave up trying to untangle her curls. "But these turquoise oceans feel all dried up about now."

Ten minutes later, the elaborate door chime rang through the house, and Natasha rushed to answer it. She fussed over Alice and Steve, took their coats and then asked if they wanted some tea. Sara's heart plummeted. This was exactly what she dreaded would happen. It was most likely nothing to worry about, and now all her friends were concerned and she was the center of attention.

"I wish I could curl up in a ball and disappear."

Bethany gave her a side hug and then rushed over to greet Alice. "Thanks for coming. I hope we didn't spoil any big plans for you guys."

"Of course not." Alice kissed her niece. "But I thought you were at the movies."

"This was more important. Todd and his buddy dropped me here instead, and I promised to fill him in later."

Alice glanced at her fiancé. "I'm sure Steve didn't mind a break from an evening of wedding planning. Flowers aren't really his passion. Right, honey?"

Steve mouthed, "Thank you," behind Alice's back, which earned him a playful swipe.

"The flowers will wait." Alice hurried over to the sofa and sank down next to Sara. "You look shaken up, sweetie. Are you feeling okay? I know you have already explained to the girls, but can you tell us exactly what's going on?"

Sara took a steadying breath. "I'm so sorry, all of you. This is the last thing I wanted to happen. It's probably a fuss about nothing, but now I guess we should talk about it and see if I should forget it or report it."

Steve made himself comfortable on the rug in front of the fireplace. "Okay. So you think someone is harassing you online, right?"

Natasha butted in. "He sent twenty-six messages in the past six months. Such a creep."

Alice gasped. "Oh, my goodness, why ever didn't you say anything before, Sara? This must be driving you crazy."

Sara shrugged. "It was gradual at first, only once in a while, and completely non-threatening. I deleted them and emptied my computer trash right away, probably because it helped me to put it out of my mind for the most part. I tried not to let it get to me, but they're coming more frequently now, and it's getting kind of creepy."

"Do you mind me asking what he writes?" Steve scooted closer to the coffee table.

"That's the weird thing." Sara stood abruptly and began pacing. "It's nothing horrific, you know? Sometimes it's something like, 'blue is your color,' or 'lame song.' I don't feel as if my life is in danger or anything, but it's unnerving. Some days he knows what clothes I've worn, and once when a bunch of us all went out for pizza, he messaged me that night saying something like, 'I didn't know mice ate pizza'. Silly stuff like that."

"Mice?" Alice's eyebrows shot up.

"Yeah, he calls me his shy little mouse. He's the eagle and I'm the prey." Sara shuddered.

Steve whistled. "Natasha said you received a message today. Mind if I take a look?"

"Please do." Sara walked back to the coffee table and slid her laptop across the glass. "I really don't want to get the police involved or tell my parents, unless you think I should. I want it all to go away. Everything else in my life is completely amazing, but this is kind of dragging me down. I hate being so fearful."

Alice took hold of Sara's hand and gently pulled her down onto the sofa. "Sweetie, have you seen anyone following you, or do you ever feel like you're being watched? I don't want to frighten you, but sometimes people get fixations on celebrities."

"I'm hardly a celebrity." Sara attempted a smile.

"You are," Bethany insisted. "You're a local celebrity for sure, and look how many magazines have published articles about you already. Your song is played on the Christian radio station all the time, Sara. I know you want to try to stay as real as possible, finishing up at your regular high school and everything, but you're getting to be pretty famous. Especially here in San Francisco."

Natasha dragged her hands down her face and grimaced. "I know I keep saying this, but I really hope this isn't our fault. I insisted Mother use all her contacts to get Sara's name out there, and she's been pushing the new songs in the Christian community. I think you're going to be famous in a lot more places than San Francisco."

"And I'm thankful, really I am." Sara sighed. "I'm sorry, you guys. I don't want to drag you all into this. I'm sure it's harmless enough—it could even be some loner in school. Maybe I should report it to the police tomorrow and try to put it behind me."

Steve closed the laptop. "Wow, that really is weird. Too bad you erased all the others though. This *Eagle* character certainly wants to freak you out, Sara. I'm glad it's nothing too sinister, but calling you his prey is pushing things a bit far for a random admirer. The fact that he's tracking you worries me. He's probably some lonely kid who thinks you're pretty and wants to be your number one fan or something."

Natasha grunted. "He's going the wrong way about getting her attention, that's for sure. He could end up being in big trouble with the police."

Sara grimaced. "Do I really have to involve the police, Steve? What do you think? I don't want to freak out my parents with this. You know how they can be."

Alice reached over and grabbed Steve's arm. "Steve, what about your friend, Jed? Isn't he posted at our local police station now?"

"Hmm, he might be able to help. Good thinking, honey." Steve looked over at Sara. "Are you comfortable with me speaking to Jed? He's a family friend and I've known him forever. He recently moved back to the area and wants to join our church. I could fill him in about this Eagle character and see what he thinks. He may know someone in their tech division who could even take a look at your laptop or something, without making a formal complaint and kicking up too much fuss."

Sara nodded. "Sure. If you don't mind."

Alice placed a hand over Sara's. "You can't let this person ruin everything you have worked so hard for. God is bigger than this, and He'll walk you through it. But in the meantime, I think you're right. First thing in the morning, Steve can put a call in to Jed. After that, you can decide if you want to share the news with your parents or keep it low key for now. Okay?"

Sara smiled, feeling a surge of courage well in the

pit of her stomach. "Thanks, you're absolutely right. This mouse isn't going to be hiding away in a little hole anytime soon."

~ *Four* ~

*S*aturday morning dawned clear and crisp. Sara barely slept a wink all night, but after a latte and her favorite breakfast of blueberry muffins and yogurt, she looked forward to spending the day helping Alice with wedding paraphernalia.

"Thanks for the ride, Mister Smithson-Blair. I think a day at Alice's place will take my mind off all this craziness." Sara smiled from the back of the Porsche.

"Oh, he doesn't mind one bit. Do you, Daddy?" Natasha turned to her father from the passenger seat.

"Of course I don't mind. And Sara, you know you only have to say the word and I'll look into this stalker business with the police. I realize Steve is going the subtler route, but I have contacts, too. You might not be my own daughter, but I feel somewhat protective and responsible for you these days."

Sara stared out at the steady pace of traffic. "Thank you. I really appreciate the way you and Mrs. Smithson-Blair took the news. I won't blame you one bit if you ask me to move back home with my parents. You've all been incredibly kind to me. The last thing I want to do is cause any stress."

"Nonsense." Natasha huffed. "For goodness sake Sara, how many times do we have to tell you? You are family now, and we stick together. Right, Daddy?"

"Absolutely, although I don't feel entirely comfortable keeping this news from your parents. If it comes up when they call next, I think we'll have to explain everything. Don't you?"

"Yes." Sara bit her lip. "Let's hope it doesn't come to that. They don't phone me very often, but I have a feeling this news won't go down well. They've always been weird about my faith, and Mom never has anything good to say about church. She'll probably blame this whole thing on God. It's such a shame they're uncomfortable with the Gracelight contract."

"Except for the money." Natasha turned in her seat and winked at Sara.

"Okay, princesses, we're here. Give me a call when you need a ride home. I'm taking my beautiful wife out for lunch later, but after that I'll be in the office downtown. Try to put this aside and have some fun, okay?"

"Thanks." The girls grabbed their purses and climbed from the car.

Sara gazed at Alice's home with a sigh. "I love this place. It reminds me of a gingerbread house."

Natasha grabbed Sara's arm. "Come on, we have some wedding flowers to give our expert opinions on."

Before they could ring the bell, the bright red door swung open and Bethany pulled both girls inside. "Come on in, it's freezing out there."

After her parents' tragic accident, Bethany moved in with her Aunt Alice, and now this was home for her, too.

Sara walked into the warm entranceway. The first time she met Bethany was here, right after the accident. It was a time when emotions were very raw, before faith was part of Bethany's life.

So much has happened since then.

"How are you doing today?" Bethany asked Sara, while she grabbed their coats and scarves, and hung them in the closet. "Did you get much sleep after all the drama?"

"Oh, I can't complain." Sara shrugged. "I'm sorry about wrecking everyone's Friday night plans."

Alice poked her head around the kitchen door. "You didn't wreck anything, and there is nothing to be sorry about. Steve phoned earlier and said he would pop into the police station to chat with Jed this morning, but I think it would be a good idea to spend the day thinking about things other than that wretched *Eagle*. What do you say, girls?"

Natasha planted a hand on one slender hip. "Let me guess, should we talk about a certain upcoming wedding instead?"

Alice grinned. "If you insist..."

The girls groaned, but ended up in a fit of giggles. The excitement of being in the wedding party was almost palpable, and in reality they were almost as giddy as Alice about the New Year's Eve wedding.

Alice shooed them from the kitchen. "Go on in by the fire, and I'll bring the hot chocolate."

Sara found her favorite spot on the comfortable couch, and tucked her legs under her. "There's something about this house in winter. It's super cozy and feels Christmassy, even in November."

"That's probably because of all the cinnamon candles she has burning." Natasha sniffed the air. "Sure smells like Christmas."

Sara noticed Bethany was gazing into the flames of the fireplace, lost in a daydream. Christmas was especially hard for her. She lost her parents on her birthday trip to see the Nutcracker ballet two years ago, and December held many painful memories. Sara's heart squeezed and she prayed silently for her friend.

Alice joined them by the fire, and set a tray on the glass coffee table. Steaming mugs of hot chocolate and a plate of chocolate chip cookies caught the attention of all three girls, and they claimed a mug and a cookie each.

"You made these, right, Beth?" Natasha held up a cookie.

Alice laughed. "Don't worry, you're perfectly safe. Bethany did all the baking. But I'll have you know, I'm slowly improving. Lucky for Steve." She tossed her thick, long hair over her shoulder and turned to Sara. "What's the latest with Gracelight? Do you have any big concerts lined up for Christmastime?"

Sara took a sip of her drink, and licked the whipping cream from her top lip. "It looks like we have a couple of concerts booked. They are supposed to confirm this week. But the thing I'm absolutely dreading is the photo shoot."

"The what?" Natasha shrieked. She quickly placed her mug on a coaster. "How is this the first I've heard about a photo shoot? You live with me, and you know I'm all over stuff like that."

Bethany snorted. "Maybe that's why she didn't mention it."

"How exciting." Alice grabbed a cookie and knelt by the fire. "Tell us the details. Who is your photographer? I might know them."

Sara glanced at the beautiful, framed photographs scattered around the living room. "I forgot you're a photographer as well as a writer. I'm not sure what his name is, but I think he's some local guy Gracelight always uses. It really is a nightmare for me—I'm the least delicate person I know. I'm bound to fall over or break something. And to be quite honest, I'm petrified."

"What?" Natasha shrieked again, even louder. "Why? You'll have a professional photographer, make-up artist, wardrobe consultant, and hairdresser all fussing around you making you look completely fabulous. I can't think of anything better."

"I can't think of anything worse." Sara groaned. "This is the part of the music industry I loathe. I wish I could simply sing and make music. A recording studio suits me perfectly. You all know how much I hate attention. I'm going to be completely awkward and I'll blush the whole time."

Bethany patted Sara's hand. "It won't be so bad. What's the photo shoot for, promotions or something?"

Sara shrugged. "I know they want to take a winter

shoot for next year's Christmas album. I guess they have to think ahead and work with the seasons."

The fireplace crackled while they all sipped their drinks in comfortable silence, each lost in thoughts of photo shoots, Christmas, and weddings.

"Wait a minute, I might have an idea." Alice set her mug on the coffee table and picked up her laptop. The girls watched her tap away on the keys. "Yes, I thought so." She squealed.

"What is it, Aunt Alice? You're killing us here." Bethany crouched next to her and glared at the screen. "Oh, my. You didn't tell me about this. How cool is that?"

Natasha growled. "Care to share?"

Alice flipped the laptop lid closed and sat cross-legged. "Okay. Here's the thing. I was given a last-minute assignment by my magazine, but I wasn't sure whether I should take it or not, with the wedding planning and everything."

"Where's the assignment?" Sara asked.

Alice grinned. "Up in Canada at some ski resort. They want a specific feature piece for the travel section, including a photo spread and everything. I was hesitant because it's for three days right at the beginning of December, and I knew I'd be in panic mode with wedding stuff by then."

"Not necessarily." Bethany rubbed her hands together. "If we all help you now, you could be organized enough to take a few days away. It sounds like fun."

"I think it might be a win-win actually." Alice winked at Sara. "It's a long shot, excuse the pun, but how would you feel about me doing your winter photo shoot?"

"Seriously?" Sara could hardly breathe. "Do you think Gracelight would allow that? Would you mind?"

Alice laughed. "First things first. I would be honored, of course. I could call Gracelight and chat with them about it. I've met Megan before, and I think they'll be familiar with my work because I'm local."

Bethany squealed. "Oh yes, you're well known in the magazine industry, and they would know your boss for sure."

"Exactly. And if we can get it all arranged, I can do my assignment alongside your shoot, and we can have some fun while we're there."

"What about us?" Natasha pouted. "Beth and I could be your assistants or something, couldn't we?"

"I would love that." Alice turned to her niece. "A December getaway might be good for us all."

Bethany smiled. "I've never been to Canada. It does sound like an interesting trip."

Alice jumped up. "Okay, I have some phone calls to make before we get carried away. Gracelight, Natasha's parents, and Sara's parents, too."

The doorbell chimed, making them all jump out of their skin. "Oh, my. Steve—yes, I should probably run it by my fiancé." A blushing Alice scampered to the front door, leaving the girls stunned.

"Do you really think we could pull this off?" Sara's heart pattered. "I mean, if Gracelight is okay with it, do you think your parents would be on board, Natasha?"

"Just let them try and stop me. Come to think of it, they'll probably foot the bill for everyone." Natasha furrowed her brow. "I'm more concerned about your parents. We'll have to make sure they know it's for your music career, not a fun trip."

Sara grinned. "But it would be a fun trip, wouldn't it?"

"Oh, you have no idea."

"What's all this?" Steve stood with his hands on his hips, attempting to look serious. "A girls' trip up north? Sounds terribly boring to me."

Bethany sighed. "Then it's a good job you aren't actually invited. You would hate it anyway—the ski slopes, picturesque mountains, ice-skating, shopping, and restaurants. You should probably stay home and look after the Youth Group or something."

"Hmm." Steve nodded. "I probably should. I suppose you want me to look after your precious little dog, too?"

Bethany gasped. "Muffin. I didn't even think of him."

Hearing his name, the little fluff-ball trotted into the living room and jumped onto Bethany's lap.

"Thanks, Steve, you're a life-saver."

"Our hero." Alice sighed and pecked his stubbly cheek. "Talking about heroes, did you talk with Jed already?"

Steve grabbed one of the cookies from the plate. "Yes, I caught him first thing. He's more than happy to help and said he'd call one of the techies downtown later today. I'll pick up your laptop this evening, Sara, and drop it back to you once they have finished with it."

"Oh, I'm in no hurry to have it back. Sometimes I wish social media hadn't been invented. I'm sure it wasn't this frazzling for singers back in the day." Sara sighed.

"I don't know about that." Natasha raised an eyebrow. "Famous people have always had issues with crazy fans and stuff. If someone wants to stalk you, they'll find a way."

"You're right, Nat." Bethany passed the plate around. "But now it's all so easy. And I think online attacks hurt many more people. There's no filter, it's instant, and pretty much anyone can be a target—you don't even have to be famous."

"I only hope it stays online. You don't suppose this *Eagle* might be actually following me, do you?" Sara's eyes stung with tears. "I mean, I know there was that comment about the pizza place, but he could have picked up on a Facebook status or something. Oh my goodness, I've been trying to keep it at the back of my mind, but this could really be dangerous, couldn't it?"

Steve brushed cookie crumbs from his coat. "Sara, I think we need to be sensible. We did the right thing by notifying the police, and I think you should keep all your social media personal comments to a minimum, at least for now."

"Yeah." Natasha nodded. "That goes for us, too, Beth. We'll have to start being really careful about what we write to her, and not give any personal stuff away. Daddy's paranoid about the security on all my accounts, but sometimes I don't think about who might be hacking or reading my comments. It's creepy."

"Can I suggest something?" Alice perched on the arm of the sofa. "I feel really awkward about keeping your parents in the dark about this, Sara. I know they might freak out, but they would freak out more if they thought you were keeping something like this secret from them. If they find out from another source, it will be even worse."

Sara stood and started pacing. "I know, I know. I hoped it might blow over, but you're right. I can't ignore this. I have to do something before it escalates. They're my parents, and even though we have a strained sort of relationship, they need to know if I'm in danger. Even if it's because of a cowardly cyber-bully."

"Want me to come with you?" Alice sipped her drink. "We could go tomorrow after church? Maybe we could suggest the photo shoot in Canada as an opportunity to take a break from all this. Do you think there's any chance they'll be agreeable?"

Sara bit her bottom lip. "I really don't know. They can be kind of unpredictable. But I guess we won't know unless we try. We need their permission for the trip anyway."

Steve leaned in for one more cookie for the road, kissed his fiancé, and saluted the girls. "I have to head off to a meeting, but I'll see you all later."

"Bye, honey. I'm going to call Gracelight right this minute." Alice picked up her phone and smiled at the girls. "I'll hide in the kitchen and leave you all to do your bridesmaid duties. Oh, and you might want to start praying about all this."

Sara took a deep breath. "No kidding."

"We were supposed to not worry about *The Eagle* nonsense today." Natasha collected Alice's bridal folder from the floor and set in on the coffee table. "Come on, bridesmaids, we have flowers to confirm and favors to wrap."

"Nat's right." Bethany pulled Sara back down onto the sofa and gabbed a basket overflowing with white tulle, pale pink ribbon, and heart-shaped chocolates. "This will help take your mind off stalkers."

"That's true. I have a stack of homework to finish this evening, but I think the least I can do is be a good bridesmaid."

Natasha grunted. "I'm so relieved she didn't want us to wear some hideous, frilly dresses."

"Alice has impeccable taste." Sara held one of the chocolates up. "Oh my goodness, even the candy wrappers are the same shade of soft pink as our dresses. And they have their names and the wedding date on them." She sighed. "It's going to be such a gorgeous wedding."

Bethany found the scissors and started cutting lengths of ribbon. "I love how our dresses are all the same shade, but slightly different in style. Kind of like us." She grinned.

"So, Beth, how many days until you start dating Todd officially?" Natasha smirked.

"Nat." Bethany dropped the scissors. "That's a bit off topic. And do you really think I would be counting the days?"

"Yes," Sara and Natasha replied in unison.

"Oh, am I really that obvious?"

"Yes." The second answer in unison caused major giggles.

Bethany pouted. "I can't help it. You guys know how head over heels I've been for what—almost two whole years?"

"Is it really that long?" Sara whistled. "I remember the first time you two met. It was after your accident, and Steve recruited Todd and me from Youth Group to paint your bedroom as a surprise. Todd was totally smitten right from the beginning."

Natasha used some of the ribbon to tie her hair into a low ponytail, and she began to sift through Alice's wedding files. "The flower section must be here somewhere. To be honest, Beth, I don't know why Alice insisted you wait until you turn sixteen to start dating. What difference does it make? You two are going to end up married anyway."

Bethany fanned her face. "I honestly hope so. We've both prayed about it. I know I'm incredibly young to be looking that far ahead, and I'm grateful Aunt Alice suggested I wait to date until I hit sixteen. I don't feel like I've missed out on anything."

"Isn't Todd seventeen already?" Sara asked.

"Yeah, only just. I'm one of the youngest in eleventh grade. My parents used to say I was ready for school when I was born, so they squeezed me in early. Todd lost out on some of his schooling when he was on the streets, but he's worked really hard to catch up. He's a smart guy."

"So he graduates this summer?" Natasha gave up looking for flower brochures and ate another cookie.

"Yeah. How cool is that?"

"I can't even imagine dating right now." Sara closed her eyes for a moment. "I wouldn't have the time. And I'm already seventeen. How about you, Natasha? You've been pretty quiet on the boy scene recently."

Natasha wrinkled her nose. "Boys are gross."

"Right." Bethany laughed. "Nat, you dated nearly every boy in our class in eighth grade."

"It's slim pickings at a school for the arts when you're in ballet, Beth. Besides, can you really call it dating when your parents have to give you a ride and pay for everything?" She sat cross-legged on the floor. "I'm waiting until God picks out someone mature and handsome and generous and loving and strong and attentive."

"Not picky at all then." Bethany threw a spool of ribbon at her friend.

"You know me." Natasha struck a pose. "What about you though, Sara? I know you're super busy, but isn't there anyone intriguing out there?"

"No, definitely not." Sara stared at the heart-shaped chocolate in her hand. The only one out there she was concerned about was her stalker. *The Eagle* consumed her thoughts, but certainly not out of intrigue.

It was pure fear.

~ *Five* ~

"*A*re you ready to go, Sara?"

The Sunday morning church service was over, and Alice started the engine of her beloved Beetle. She turned to Sara in the passenger seat, who clutched her purse with a death grip.

"Your parents know we're coming, right?"

"Yes, I checked to make sure they were going to be home. They even offered to make us a quick lunch, if that's okay with you, Alice."

"Oh, of course. Did you hear my stomach rumbling for the last ten minutes of the sermon? I was mortified."

Alice carefully pulled out of the church parking lot and into the sparse flow of traffic. "I hate to ask, but have you received any more messages from *The Eagle* since Friday? I know your parents will want to know."

Sara pulled at her long ringlets, and wound one around her finger. "No, nothing since Friday. I wonder if there's any way he could know the police looked at my social media accounts. Maybe it will scare him off."

"That would certainly be a nice solution."

Alice turned up the radio and hummed along to a Hillsong tune. "Hey, when is your CD release date?"

Sara smiled. "We still have some recording to do over the winter months, but I think they're hoping for a spring release. Then it'll be time to work on the album for next Christmas. I'm already excited about that."

"Megan, at Gracelight, certainly thinks the world of you. I still can't believe how easy it was to make arrangements for your photo shoot. She was very accommodating, and seemed genuinely excited about the shoot in Canada."

"Megan's the best. And now that I have you to take

36

care of my photo shoot, it's absolutely perfect. I'll write thank you cards this week to Megan and to your boss, too. Now we just have to convince my parents."

The San Francisco winter sunshine streamed through the car windows, causing Sara to squint. Her heart's rhythm sped up a little when they turned onto the street where her parents and brothers lived. Where *she* lived up until a few short months ago. Why were her palms sweating?

"You okay?" Alice pulled up outside the doublewide trailer. "You're awfully quiet. I met your family before, you know. It's going to be fine. You do the talking, I'll be there for moral support and to answer any questions they might have."

Sara nodded and unbuckled her seatbelt. "Sure, but I apologize in advance for anything my mom might say. I can't believe how nervous I am about speaking with my own parents. I only moved out a little while ago, but it seems like I never even lived here. How weird is that?"

She observed the worn-out neighborhood with fresh eyes. It all looked exhausted and in desperate need of repair, although her mother made a minor improvement on their place, by giving the front door a fresh coat of red paint. An assortment of toys littered the small front yard, and Sara's eyes blurred with tears when she thought of her little brothers. She missed them dearly, and was concerned about them falling in with the wrong crowds one day.

"I worry about James, you know. He's the oldest and we used to be close. Since I moved out, he's been distant and angry. I hope he's not getting into trouble."

A large group of young teens huddled on the browning lawn opposite, and passed around either cigarettes or pot. Sara shuddered. She opened the car door and turned back to Alice.

"Let's do this."

Before Sara could swing her purse over her shoulder,

she heard high-pitched screams. Her two youngest brothers raced down the short driveway and hurled themselves at her.

"Sara, we missed you!"

"Why don't you come and visit every day?"

"When are you coming home to live with us again?"

Alice observed the huddle and laughed. "I wish I had brothers."

With that, the middle one, Jake, hurried over to give Alice some attention while Timothy, the youngest, clung tightly to his big sister.

"I miss you," he whispered.

Sara picked up the six-year-old and twirled him in her arms. "When did you get so tall, tiny Tim?"

"I'm not tall. James and Jake are tall. They say I'm a baby."

"Nonsense. Where is James anyway?" Sara scanned the front yard.

"Right here."

Sara spun around. James stomped across the street, away from the group of kids who were smoking. Her heart plummeted.

"James, how are you?" Sara hugged her brother, and he halfheartedly patted her back.

"Good."

She tipped her head toward the guys on the lawn. "New friends?"

"Sort of. Don't worry, sis, I'm not smoking if that's what you're worried about."

Without waiting for a reply he dug his hands deeper in the pockets of his baggy jeans, and stalked off toward the front door.

Sara's pulse quickened. "Oh, James."

"What's wrong, Sara?" Timothy looked at her with wide eyes.

Sara shrugged. "I guess he's getting all pre-teen on

us."

Jake stared down at his scruffy tennis shoes. "Yeah. He doesn't ever want to hang out with us anymore. He says we're not cool enough."

"I think you're both super cool. James doesn't know what he's missing. Go on inside where it's nice and warm, boys. I'll be right there."

She grabbed Alice's hand and pulled her close. "Something's not right with James. He knows better than to hang with the wrong crowd. And I've seen too many good kids mess up their lives in this neighborhood. I have a horrible feeling about this."

Alice squeezed Sara's hand. "Try not to worry. Maybe we can invite him to Youth, and Steve can get to know him. Don't lose hope, sweetie. Besides, we have things to discuss with your parents first. Are you ready?"

Sara's throat was bone dry, so she merely nodded.

Mrs. Dean stood inside the cramped entrance and awkwardly welcomed Sara inside. "Come on in before we freeze to death." Her voice was monotone and void of any emotion. "I know it's not as fancy as what you're used to now, but it's our little home sweet home."

"Mom, you know I love coming here to see you, but please don't start being funny about me staying with Natasha. It's really convenient being closer to school and the studio, and it helps me keep up with the schedule. The Smithson-Blairs have been so kind."

The littlest brothers dragged Alice through the door, and she held a hand out to Mrs. Dean. "So good to see you again. How are you and your husband?"

Sara's mother ignored the outstretched hand and wandered into the tiny living room. "Well as can be expected."

Sara shrugged out of her blue, wool jacket and hung it on a peg, along with Alice's coat. "Where's Dad?"

"He'll be home any minute. Come on in and sit, both

of you. Sara said you have something to talk about."

Sara, Alice, and all three boys poured into the room, and suddenly Sara felt claustrophobic.

Did I feel like this when I lived here?

"Sara?" Timothy squeezed her hand. "You look pale."

She shook her head. "I'm fine. A bit warm, that's all."

Mrs. Dean sighed. "Boys, your sister's forgotten what it's like to live in a stuffy trailer. Go and play outside and look out for your father. He should be here by now."

Grumbling and kicking at one another, the younger two disappeared outside, and James ran to his room. An awkward silence prevailed.

"Can I make some tea, Mom?" Sara stood. "I'm sure you'd like a cup."

"Might as well make yourself useful. You know where everything is."

Sara glanced at Alice and grimaced. She stepped into the kitchen, which was so close she could hear the conversation in the living room.

"Those boys are growing up fast, Mrs. Dean. How old is James now? He must be nearly old enough to come to our Youth Group."

"He's eleven, and getting into that preteen, moody phase. Always looks at you like he's up to no good. Jake's nine-and-a-half, and not much better. They're monsters most of the time. Not sure you would want him at your nice little church."

Sara cringed. Her mother never liked the church and used every opportunity possible to grumble about it.

"Oh, nonsense." Alice chuckled. "We have a whole bunch of little monsters who attend, and we love every single one of them."

While Alice explained the youth program, Sara listened from the kitchen sink.

Alice is so forgiving, so gracious and open toward everyone she meets. She's stunningly beautiful on the outside, but that's nothing compared to the beauty that radiates from within. That's how I want to be one day.

"Hello, sweetheart." A male voice boomed from the entrance porch, pulling Sara from her musings. "Got a hug for your poor old dad?"

"Dad!" Sara rushed to embrace her father, relishing the familiar scent of Old Spice and tobacco. "Do you want some tea? I'm making a pot."

"Sure, that sounds perfect." He dumped his rain jacket on a chair, waved at the ladies in the living room, and limped over to join Sara in the kitchen. "We made sandwiches earlier. Nothing fancy I'm afraid. I'll set them on the coffee table."

"Thanks, Dad." Her eyes almost brimmed over with gratitude. Where her mother was awkward and self-conscious with people—even her own family, her father was relaxed and conversational with almost everyone. "How's the leg these days?"

"Oh, you know. The cold weather doesn't help, but there's no point grumbling. How's my singing angel?"

"Pretty good." Sara carried the tray into the living room. "All things considered."

The four of them congregated around the scratched-up coffee table, with a tray of mismatched mugs and a plate of egg sandwiches to share.

"Are the boys coming in to join us?" Alice peered through the front window.

Mr. Dean's laugh was infectious. "I think it's best we have our fill, and let the locusts come and finish it off afterwards. They'll be fine out there for a few minutes. They're having a game of tag or something. Anyway, your mother says you have something to talk about, Sara. Is everything okay at school?" He took a loud swig of tea.

"School's fine. My grades are still at the top, and I'm

managing to fit my singing around homework and everything."

"I should hope so." Mrs. Dean folded her arms. "Edu-
cation is important. You don't want to end up like us, do
you?"

Sara's shoulders slumped. This was going to be hard
work. She took a bracing breath and continued. "I hope this
is nothing and I don't want to worry you, but I think you
ought to know that someone is harassing me."

Mr. Dean slammed down his mug. "Who?"

Sara tried not to frown or look worried. "Don't get
upset, Dad, it's not physical. It's probably someone simply
bugging me but he's been sending some messages on social
media and email to try to unnerve me."

"I never trust the Internet." Mrs. Dean shook her
head, then looked into Sara's eyes with the most concern
the girl had seen in years. Maybe even since the tragic
death of Sara's baby brother, almost four years ago. "Is he
threatening you, Sara?"

Sara reached out and touched her mother's rough,
pale hand. "No, Mom. It's nothing like that. He's never
given a hint of violence or anything. It's more creepy stuff.
He knows where I've been sometimes, and he insults my
singing, and says mean things about me being so shy and
nervous. I'm sure I'm not in any physical danger. It's a bit
worrying, that's all."

"I don't like the sound of it." Mr. Dean stood, and
paced the worn carpet with his pronounced limp. Sara suddenly realized where she got her pacing gene. "If anyone
ever hurt you, Sara, they would have me to deal with. Do
you think we should involve the police?"

Sara looked desperately at Alice, hoping she would
explain.

"Mister and Mrs. Dean, you have to know that I only
found out about this on Friday night. Your daughter has
been carrying this weight on her shoulders for months,

and obviously we want to help her. My fiancé, Steve—"

"The youth pastor?" Mrs. Dean almost spat the words out.

"Yes, he has a good friend named Jed in the local police office. Jed ran a check on Sara's laptop. We hope to get the results either today or tomorrow. But there has been no attempt by this individual to contact Sara outside of cyberspace."

"Coward." Sara's father wrung his hands while he paced. "It's this cyber-bullying nonsense, isn't it? People these days think they have the right to say whatever they want behind the protection of a screen—even when it's cruel and damaging. It's not right. Are you really okay, sweetheart?"

Sara's heart melted at the sight of her father's face, etched with worry lines. She nodded. If she tried to speak right now the tears would come. A wonky smile would have to do.

Mrs. Dean pointed a gnarly finger at Sara. "This singing career brought it on. You were perfectly safe here until you decided to be famous and went to stay with that hoity-toity friend in her mansion. No wonder you have cyber-stalkers after you. You're a quiet girl, Sara, you should be happy with a quiet life."

Silence filled the stifling room. Sara replayed that last sentence over and over while Alice cleared her throat.

You're a quiet girl, Sara, you should be happy with a quiet life.

"That's not fair." Sara's father collapsed onto the sofa. "You know our daughter has a gift. She has a voice like an angel, and we might not understand God like she does, but if she chooses to use her talent singing those Christian songs, then we should support her. It could be a lot worse."

His wife huffed and looked through the front window in the direction of her sons.

Alice turned toward Mrs. Dean. "Look, I know you must be worried. I promise we're doing everything we can to protect Sara, and get this online nonsense stopped. In fact, there's something else we want to ask you. Right, Sara?"

Sara sipped the tea. She needed a moment to steady herself for the next inevitable barrage of insults. She cleared her throat. "Mom... Dad... Gracelight want me to do a photo shoot for next year's Christmas album cover."

Her mother stifled a laugh. "Funny how we could never get you to be in any photographs before. Now, suddenly, you're a model."

"Mary, will you please give her chance to speak? You will have no problem accepting the money she earns from the folks at Gracelight." Mr. Dean was getting impatient, and Sara's shoulders began to tense.

"It's okay, Dad. Mom's right—I absolutely hate having my photo taken. Always have and probably always will. But that's where Alice comes in." She smiled at her friend before continuing. "We spoke with my manager at Gracelight, and they are happy for Alice to be my photographer."

Mr. Dean slapped his forehead. "Of course, you're a writer and a photographer. Sara has a few of your magazine pieces here somewhere, Alice. I forgot about that. I'm sure she'll feel a lot more comfortable posing in front of a friend's camera than some stranger. Sounds like a great idea."

Alice leaned forward. "We are both thrilled. But I have to explain that I'll be doing the shoot in British Columbia, and it'll be next weekend. I apologize for the short notice, but we are combining it with a pre-arranged assignment."

"British Columbia in Canada?" Sara's mother raised both brows.

"I have the details right here." Alice delved into her purse and pulled out a brochure along with an itinerary and

44

permission forms. "I know this is a bombshell to drop on you now, but I can leave these with you to look over."

Sara's parents sat together and skimmed the information.

"Can I go? It's all paid for." Sara held her breath.

"How much school will you miss?" Mrs. Dean pursed her lips.

"Only one day, Mom. We'll fly out Friday early evening, and come home on Monday morning. I'll be back in class on Tuesday, and I can take any homework with me. Natasha and Bethany are planning on coming, too."

"What about a passport?"

"It's okay, Mom, I got one for the Mexico mission's trip earlier this year, remember?"

Mrs. Dean shrugged.

"Please?" Sara was not too proud to beg.

"Sounds like fun." Her father winked. "I think it's a wonderful opportunity. Never been to Canada myself. I'll sign these forms for you. Got a pen, Mary?"

Mrs. Dean huffed again and pulled a pen from a tiny drawer in the coffee table.

"Thanks, Mom and Dad, you don't know how much this means to me."

Alice stood. "I have a few errands to run, but why don't I pop back for you in an hour, Sara? It'll give you time to catch up with your family."

Sara couldn't wipe the silly grin from her face. "Thanks, Alice. I would love that. I feel like I could burst with happiness right now."

Her mother scowled. "Let's hope your cyber-stalker doesn't decide to follow you up north."

~ *Six* ~

"*H*ey, Natasha, it's Sara. Everyone is talking about the photo shoot at my school today. How crazy is that? I can't believe how quickly news spreads in this place. I'm totally embarrassed. Are we still on for tea at Alice's place? Text me, and hopefully, I'll see you at four. Bye."

Sara checked her phone for any new messages, and then tucked it into her jeans' pocket. She started school early this morning for a math tutorial, and missed her usual chat with Natasha at breakfast. Being absent for the odd class due to her singing was acceptable, but she didn't want to fall behind on her studies, and therefore took advantage of any additional classes she could attend.

"You're so conscientious."

Sara spun around from her locker, and was face to face with Adam Tromness, the most popular boy in her class. Heat crept up her neck beneath her collared shirt—a sure sign her cheeks were glowing.

"I saw you come out of the extra math class, Sara Dean. First thing on a Monday morning? You are definitely way too conscientious."

"Hey, Adam. Yeah, I guess I am. Do you have science next?" In an attempt to appear nonchalant, Sara slung her backpack casually over her shoulder, and hit him hard in the ribs. He doubled over and feigned injury.

"Oh, I'm so sorry, Adam. I'm such a klutz." She glanced around, hoping nobody else noticed, but of course several students watched with mouths wide open. Someone even snapped a photo on a phone. "Unbelievable," she muttered.

Adam straightened with a grin and touched her arm. "No harm done. I have plenty of ribs." He suddenly saw the crowd of onlookers. "Wow, looks like you have quite the following these days. Come on, I'll walk you to science."

Sara dipped her head and hurried through the corridor, desperate to escape the attention. They slowed their pace once the crowd thinned, and Sara's breathing returned to normal. "I really am sorry. For the ribs and the show."

Adam laughed. "Are you kidding? That little episode took me up a notch in the popularity ratings. I might be up somewhere close to you now."

Sara cringed.

"What? You don't like being popular?" Adam's eyebrows shot up, making him look completely adorable. "You're a famous singer in these parts, you know. Not just a nerdy shy girl with a nice voice."

Sara blew a curl from her face and stopped outside the classroom. "Actually, no, I don't like being popular. You probably think that's weird, but I really am that nerdy, shy girl with a nice voice. I got signed up, and now suddenly everyone wants to know me." She lowered her voice to a near whisper. "You never even spoke to me before today, Adam, and that's okay. I don't blame you."

"I asked to borrow your pen once. I remember it clearly." Adam's dimples deepened on his handsome face. "I think I might have been flirting with you actually. And that was before you became all rich and famous."

Sara laughed incredulously. "I'm certainly not rich, and I'm far from famous. But thanks anyway."

Adam stuck out his hand. "Friends?"

Sara glanced around. Nobody was watching but this still felt beyond weird. Hadn't she been invisible until a few short months ago? She accepted the handshake but ensured it was curt and professional, rather than star struck and pathetic. "Sure. We should get into class before Miss West blows a gasket."

Science was slow and uneventful. Sara sensed

Adam's eyes were on her a few times during the course of the morning from his seat in the back row, but she made sure not to encourage him. At lunchtime, she caught up with homework, and then managed to focus enough to get through an afternoon of English Literature. An explication of Romeo and Juliet certainly didn't help her forget about Adam's earlier interaction.

As soon as the school buzzer sounded to mark the end of the day, Sara ran through the rain and caught the bus to Alice's house, where she shared her Adam story with the girls.

"Sara Dean." Natasha slurped her tea. "Are you serious? All the girls at our school know about *the* Adam Tromness. He's only the hottest boy out there, and he totally flirted with you. Oh, my goodness. Beth, did you hear that?"

Bethany hurried into the living room, closely followed by Muffin the fluff-ball, and set a plate of macaroons on the table. "Adam Tromness? Sara, that's wild. And you whacked him with your backpack?"

Sara bit her lip. "It was an accident. Why am I so uncoordinated? And trust me, I'm not all overcome about the whole thing. Not really. Yes, it was a little flattering at the time, but honestly, I can't believe how popular kids want to hang out with me all of a sudden." She stopped pacing.

"Did he give you his number or anything?" Natasha grabbed a raspberry macaroon from the plate. "This is so exciting. I've never heard you even utter a boy's name before."

"Absolutely not. Even if he did, I wouldn't want to date him. I'm not interested in dating anyone. I have too much on my plate as it is. Not to mention the fact that he's a total party animal."

Bethany nodded. "That's true. He doesn't have the best reputation, but well done for surviving the encounter, Sara. Are the super-popular kids really including you now?

That must be weird."

Sara peeled off her cardigan and sat in front of the fire. Muffin curled up next to her, ready for some attention. "Totally weird. I have invites to their parties and everything. It's not my thing, so I have no intention of going, but it's interesting how fickle people can be. They didn't even know my name last year."

"You are pretty quiet." Natasha cringed. "Remember how I ignored you at first. I guess I thought you wanted to be invisible, so I treated you like that." She screwed up her nose. "I was pretty beastly. It's a good thing Beth is such a nice person, otherwise you might not have stuck around."

"Oh, you weren't that bad." Sara attempted to disguise a giggle with a cough.

"Yes, she was." Bethany burst into laughter.

Natasha groaned and buried her head in a red velvet pillow.

Alice joined in the laughter from her seat at the desk under the window. "You know we all love you, Natasha."

"I know." Natasha surfaced from the pillow. "Hey, Sara, I just had a thought. You don't suppose Adam could be your stalker, do you?"

"No way. He's got no reason to be anyone's stalker. He could have his pick of any girl he likes, and even though he's a bit full of himself, he doesn't strike me as a mean person." Sara picked up a mug of hot chocolate from the coffee table and took a swig of the delicious, hot sweetness. "Mmm. Thanks for this, Alice. I feel warmer already."

"That's because you've been talking about Adam Tromness," Natasha murmured.

Alice ignored the comment. "You're very welcome." She swiveled her chair away from the desk, and faced the girls. "Sara, has word spread in school about your photo shoot yet?"

"Oh yes. That was gossip of the day. I have no idea how stuff like that leaks out. Probably why Adam decided I was worth speaking to. I kind of wish I was invisible again."

"Really?" Natasha shook her head. "Sometimes I think we should trade lives. Although singing isn't my thing, attention sure is. Why is it so bad? I don't get it."

Sara twirled a damp ringlet around her finger. "I don't know. I'm not used to it, I suppose. I'm happy being the wallflower. I like observing rather than being observed. You know I can be kind of klutzy, and I dread messing up in front of everyone. Mostly I hate feeling awkward and not being able to be myself. These new so-called friends who keep trying to include me are not really interested in who I am or what makes me tick."

"You don't know that for sure." Bethany scooted closer to Sara's side. "Besides, you may get chance to share your faith with some of them. That would be cool. You were such a huge help to me when I needed it—who knows how many others are hurting right now at your school?"

"I know, and you're right. I try to take each opportunity as it comes. It's not exactly a secret that my music is faith-based. I need to be less fearful. It's something I'm working on. But it can be tricky deciding who is a genuine friend. Thankfully, I have a few other nerdy girls in my class who I've known for years. They're not in the least bit affected by the fuss."

Bethany reached over and gave her a hug. "You'll always have us, Sara. I wish you could come to our school for the arts."

Sara shook her head. "I like my school. Remember I promised not get all weird and different when I got this contract? I think suddenly dropping out of high school and attending the most elite school for the arts in San Francisco is way too weird and different for someone like me. I want to fly under the radar as much as possible."

Bethany sighed. "At least the kids at your school are actually being nice to you, even if it's superficial. It could be worse."

"Talking of worse," Natasha brushed at a few macaroon crumbs on her sweater, "have you received any more creepy messages from *The Eagle*?"

Sara shivered in spite of the roaring fire in the hearth. "Honestly, I haven't checked all day. Half of me doesn't want to, but I know I probably should."

"Would you like to use my laptop?" Alice carried it over to the coffee table. "You might as well look with us here for support, just in case."

Sara bit her lip as she typed in details to check her email. Several messages popped up in the inbox, and she quickly scanned the list. Her breath caught in her throat.

"Oh, no."

Natasha, Bethany, and Alice surrounded Sara while she clicked on the unfamiliar address. Sara read it aloud:

"Little Miss Popular today, weren't you? Go back into your mouse hole.
The Eagle."

Bethany gasped. "That's so petty. And awful."

Alice stood abruptly. "No, wait, it's not necessarily awful. This means *The Eagle* was at your school today, right?"

"Or he knows somebody who was at your school," Natasha added. "It could be second hand news." She drummed her long, plum-colored fingernails on the laptop keyboard. "Are you absolutely sure it couldn't be gorgeous Adam?"

Sara stared at her shaking hands. She could barely feel them. Acid burned in her stomach and suddenly she needed to throw up. "Excuse me," she croaked, and sprinted to the bathroom.

She slammed the door shut, emptied the contents of her stomach down the toilet bowl, and washed her hands.

51

The warm water felt soothing, and she splashed some over her face. After several deep breaths, she felt a little more human. While soft voices talked in the living room, she gazed at her reflection. She looked even paler than usual, and a few pounds lighter, if her pronounced cheekbones were anything to go by. Her bright turquoise eyes stared back at her, sad and exhausted. They had lost their sparkle. The stress was getting to be too much, but she didn't want to let anyone down.

Lord, what am I supposed to do? Am I really in danger? I'm scared all the time, and I feel sick all the time, and this is meant to be an exciting, fabulous experience. I want to be normal and go to my normal school. I don't want people to treat me differently because I'm a singer now. And I don't want to put my friends in danger. Please help me.

Someone knocked gently on the bathroom door.

"Sara, it's Alice. How are you doing in there? Can I get you anything, sweetie?"

Sara dried her hands and opened the door. "Hey. No, I think I'm okay now, but thanks."

Alice stepped forward and enveloped Sara in a warm hug. Sara clung to her, not wanting to let go. "Alice," she whispered, "I'm scared."

Neither one moved for several minutes. Sara cried, and Alice was simply there, a soothing presence and more of a mother figure than Mrs. Dean ever was. Eventually, Sara pulled back and wiped her eyes.

"Alice, do you think we should still go away on Friday? I don't want to put any of you in danger."

"Honestly, I think it's the best thing for you to do right now. This coward seems harmless enough physically, even if he is terrorizing you mentally. If he's from your school, he can't exactly follow you to Canada. A few days away in the fresh mountain air might be good for you. I'm actually looking forward to having a weekend without wedding planning, and I know the girls are excited about the trip. But it's your call."

"We can hear you," Natasha bellowed from the living room. "And for the record, we all need a girls' trip. Not to mention the fact that I already bought some fabulous fur snow boots especially for Canada."

Sara smiled. "I guess that's decided then." She sighed and led Alice back to the sofa. "But what should we do about this stupid email today? I really don't think Adam would do a thing like this. He has a harem of doting girls at his beck and call, and there's no reason for him to follow me. It doesn't make any sense. Plus, I don't think he would have been all flirty with me this morning if he was a stalker."

"Can we ask Steve to show the message to Jed at the police station?" Bethany re-read the email. "Or even send it to him?"

Alice grabbed her phone. "I'm all over it. We'll call in at the station ourselves and I'll give you girls a ride back home. I know you'll want to get on top of your homework before our trip this weekend. If Sara is sure about going ahead with it."

"I'm sure. It's not like anyone is going to follow me to another country to freak me out. Right?"

Natasha whistled. "Let's hope not."

While Alice spoke with Steve on the phone, Bethany and Natasha quickly finished the last of the macaroons, but Sara couldn't stomach even one. Her gut felt as messed up as her life.

~ Seven ~

*A*fter all the excitement on Monday, the next three days were filled with school, homework, and packing for the trip. Steve contacted Jed at the station, and the latest email was tracked to the school area, which was a start at least. *The Eagle* was definitely a local. Sara tried to put the issue out of her mind, and the girls kept up her spirits with plans for Canada. By Thursday there were no more creepy messages, but Sara had some exciting news to share.

"Natasha, are you home?" Sara shouted into the Smithson-Blairs' foyer. She dumped her heavy backpack on the floor and swiftly shed her wool jacket. Goodness, it was cold outside. She leaned over to catch her breath, and then hung the jacket in a closet. "Natasha?"

"Where's the fire?" Natasha calmly descended the spiral staircase, engrossed with her phone. She finally glanced up. "Oh, my. Your hair is crazy. You look like you ran all the way home from school. What's wrong?"

"Oh, nothing's wrong." Sara's cheeks ached from grinning all afternoon. "But I did run all the way from the bus stop. It's freezing." She rubbed her frigid cheeks.

"Sara, is everything okay?" Natasha's mother gracefully clipped across the tiles in her signature high heels and took Sara's chilled hand in her own. "I heard you shouting. It's not that stalker nonsense is it, dear?"

Sara bit her lip. "Oh, no, I'm sorry for the fuss. Nothing's wrong. Actually, I have some exciting news."

Now she had Natasha's undivided attention. "What is it? I haven't seen you so joyful in ages. Spit it out."

Sara took a deep breath. "Megan at Gracelight phoned me at lunchtime today. It looks like I have a concert booked for this Sunday evening. In Canada."

"What?" Natasha squealed. "This Sunday? How on earth did you manage that?"

Georgia Smithson-Blair hugged Sara tightly. "I knew word would spread about your talent, my dear. Whereabouts is the concert?" Her eyes lit up. "Is it in Vancouver? I love that city. Been there numerous times."

Sara nodded. "Yes, apparently there's some big event going on with several Christian artists performing, and there happened to be a slot open due to a last minute cancellation. We were due to fly home via Vancouver anyway, but Megan managed to snag Alice and I earlier flights, so we can make the concert. That way, Alice can take some concert shots, too." She frowned. "Megan said there were several seats still available on that earlier flight if you and Bethany want to join us, Natasha."

"Duh. Of course we want to see you in concert."

"Awesome. She can get you tickets to the concert, no problem. We just need to get those flights changed. Is that cool? I said we'd confirm tonight."

Before Natasha could get a word in, her mother clipped off to the study. "Consider it done," she called behind her. "Megan and I are on first-name terms. I'll call her right now and get everything booked and arranged."

Natasha shrugged. "Then I guess Beth will have to be on board. Oh, Sara, this is beyond amazing. Are you nervous? I know how you hate being up on stage." She dragged her into the kitchen and they perched on barstools by the counter.

"Of course I'm nervous. You know how I am in front of big crowds. But I realize this is a huge part of my career, and somehow God always takes away the butterflies once I'm singing. I can't help believing He has orchestrated this whole thing."

"I think you're right. Does Alice know about the concert yet?"

"Yes. I thought I should phone her first because Megan needed to book her ticket as soon as possible. Of course, she was thrilled, and she will get extra pay for photographing the concert, too."

"I don't think she and Steve are exactly strapped for cash, you know." Natasha leaned against the counter. "His family is totally loaded. I mean serious money. And that's quite something coming from me."

Sara shrugged. "Bethany says Steve turned his back on all that when he left home and went into the ministry. I think the only handout he accepts is the Christmas celebration money. You know, the big party he throws for the youth with the sleigh rides and bonfire and all that."

"Oh, yes. His mother funds it, doesn't she? I wonder what this wedding is going to really be like. Poor Alice. I have a feeling she would prefer simple."

Sara grinned. "It's going to be fabulous. I can hardly believe we're in her bridal party. I've never even been to a wedding before."

"Really? I've been a flower girl three times and this is my second times as a bridesmaid." She sighed. "I find them rather tedious myself."

"Natasha. Really? I can't wait. By the looks of her planning books, this is going to be absolutely perfect." Sara chewed her thumbnail. "I feel a bit guilty taking her away this weekend when she only has a few weeks left before the wedding."

"I don't think she minds. It was her suggestion—remember? Want some peppermint tea?"

"Please." Sara watched Natasha flit about the kitchen in her usual ballerina style. "I wish there was something special we could do for her while we're away. Something wedding-y."

"Her bridal shower is in two weeks. Maybe mother will have some ideas. She's great at planning stuff. I'll see if she's finished on the phone with Megan."

Natasha wandered off to the study, and Sara

slumped over the counter, suddenly exhausted. Life was never boring, that was for sure. She lifted one hand above the granite counter top and watched it tremble. Was it from exhilaration or fear?

"What's all this? You want to surprise Alice?" Georgia Smithson-Blair's red hair flowed behind her as she hurried into the kitchen. She opened a drawer and pulled out a large notebook and a pen.

Natasha grinned at Sara. "She always has great ideas."

"Now, let's think carefully about this, girls. I don't know Alice terribly well, but her sister was my very best friend. I think Alice would probably appreciate something intimate and heartfelt rather than all out and flashy. Am I right?"

"Absolutely." Sara nodded.

"Hmm. Do you know if she's got the 'something old, something new, something borrowed, something blue' covered yet for the wedding day?"

"Oh, wait." Natasha slapped her hands on the counter. "This is perfect. We were talking about this on Saturday, and she only has the 'something blue' and 'something new'."

"That's right." Sara stopped chewing her nail. "The wedding dress is new, of course. And I think the blue item is a sapphire in the ring she is wearing. It belonged to her mother, apparently."

Mrs. Smithson-Blair's eyes misted over. "So much tragedy in that family. First she loses both parents in a horrific fire, and then her only sister and brother-in-law in that wretched accident."

Natasha placed a hand over her mother's. "She was her sister, but Anita was your best friend, Mother. I still can't believe they are gone."

"Me either. Bethany is such a brave girl. She's very fortunate to have Alice for an aunt, that's for sure."

Sara held back tears. "I've heard so much about Bethany's parents, I know they were very special to you all. It's going to be hard for Alice, not having any close family there at her wedding. I can't even imagine."

"Maybe we can do something about that." Georgia suddenly bolted from the room. "I'll be right back."

Natasha shook her head. "She obviously thought of something. I'll pour the tea. I'll make one for Mother, too—something tells me she's going to need it."

"Want an apple while we're waiting?" Sara picked a deep red one from the fruit bowl and held it up.

"Sure, why not."

"Okay, girls." Georgia breezed back in with a wooden box under her arm. "Tell me if I'm way off, but I think we might have something old and something borrowed right here."

Natasha carried three steaming mugs to the breakfast bar and set them down. "Whatever do you have there? I don't think I've seen that box before."

"I keep it on the top shelf of my closet, and to be quite honest, I haven't brought it down in over a year. It's still too painful. But I think this occasion calls for it."

"Can we see what's inside? Is it from Bethany's mom?"

The three of them huddled together and Georgia slowly lifted the mahogany lid. She reverently picked up the contents and placed them on the counter.

Sara gasped. "Beautiful photographs. I recognize you, Mrs. Smithson-Blair. Is that Bethany's mom there with you?" A young redheaded beauty sat on a beach alongside an equally stunning brunette.

"Yes," she whispered. "You can both take a look. We go back to when the girls were babies. You can see some shots with you and Bethany here, Natasha." They flipped through the pictures silently, until they reached an old black and white one.

58

"Mother, why do you have this one?" Natasha closely inspected the small, fragile photograph. "This must be Anita with Alice when they were little girls, and I'm guessing these are their parents."

"That's right. For some reason, Anita left a box of mementos to me in her will. Mostly these photos, but also this beautiful little frame." She held up an intricate silver frame in the light. It was encrusted with pearls and held a picture of the two beautiful friends several years ago at some fancy ball.

"It's stunning." Sara was mesmerized.

"What are you thinking about, Mother? I know you have a plan here."

Georgia smiled. "Okay. Poor Alice can't have her family there on her special day, but she needs some memory to carry with her. I think it might help. So, what if we put the picture of her with her parents and sister inside this special little silver frame, and we work it into the bouquet somehow? It should fit perfectly. That way she can carry their memory with her down the aisle. The frame is borrowed, and the photo is old."

Natasha and Sara both hugged Georgia tightly and squealed their excitement.

"Is that a 'yes' then?"

"Mother, that's genius. I know she has a gorgeous bouquet of soft pink roses and some greenery, which I am clueless about. But I think the florist could work the little frame into the ribbon and the dangly stuff, and it would be fabulous. You are a marvel."

Georgia held the frame out at arm's length and squinted at it. "I think it'll work well. I know exactly which florist she's using, because she had the good sense to ask for my recommendation. I don't know everything, but event planning is my specialty, and that means flowers. I'll give them a call right now, so we can know for sure if they can make it work—if she likes the idea, of course."

59

"She's going to love this surprise." Sara helped re-load the box of photographs, and sat with Natasha while Georgia rushed away to make the phone call.

"I love your mom."

Natasha grinned. "Me, too. She's come a long way this year. Like the rest of us."

They sipped tea and half listened to the phone call confirming the bouquet, and once it was all arranged, a phone call to Bethany was next on the agenda.

"I hadn't really thought about how emotional this wedding is going to be for Beth." Natasha bit into an apple.

"She's bound to miss her parents deeply. We'll be there for her though." Sara rolled her apple around in her hands. "Listen, this is a bit off topic, but I have something else I need to ask you and Bethany."

"Hmm?" Natasha pirouetted and landed perfectly.

"What do you think about the two of you dancing at the concert on Sunday? You could do a couple of your familiar routines during my slower numbers? It would be perfect. I know Megan from Gracelight would jump all over it." Sara chewed her fingernail. "Actually, I already spoke with her about it at lunchtime."

Natasha squealed again. "Are you serious? In Vancouver? Oh, my. That would be such a great experience for us both. We could wear our peach contemporary dance dresses. They are understated, yet graceful. Are you sure? You're not just saying it to make us feel included? I know I can be needy sometimes, but this is about you."

Sara laughed and jumped off her stool. She stood in front of Natasha and held both her hands. "You are my best friends and a huge part of this journey. It'll be like that time in the seniors' home in Mexico, remember? You danced and I sang. It was magical."

Natasha snorted. "Yeah, except this time there will be hundreds in the audience, and hopefully they will all be wide awake." She fanned herself dramatically and picked up her phone from the counter. "Right, I think it's time we phoned Bethany and filled her in on a few of the important details—about the picture frame and the concert. She's totally going to freak."

Sara straightened up the kitchen while Natasha chatted with Bethany. She could hear the screams through the phone from the other side of the kitchen and she smiled. Having her friends on stage with her, even for a couple of songs, would be so special. She planned to phone Megan and confirm as soon as Bethany agreed, and then the girls would probably even get together to decide on routines later tonight. Sara inhaled. Watching her friends dance left her breathless. She could only imagine being that graceful. They were both incredibly gifted, and would end up in the professional ballet world eventually. She sighed contentedly and a peace washed over her. A peace she hadn't experienced in a long time.

Lord, You know I've been worried about my own family—especially my brother James, and I commit them to You now. But thank You so much for providing me with this family—my dearest friends, who I get to do life with. I'm petrified at the thought of the concert, but I know You will be right there with me. And I'm fearful, as usual, about the fame. The Eagle, the attention, the media, the strangers who suddenly think they are entitled to be in my life—please protect my friends and me from all harm. And thank You for blessing me beyond my wildest dreams. Amen.

~ *Eight* ~

"*H*ey Dad, it's Sara. I'm leaving a message to let you know our plane landed in Vancouver. We're in the airport right now. One more little flight and we'll be at the ski resort. Speak to you soon. Love you."

Sara stopped pacing and slid the phone into her purse. A little people-watching would help pass the time. She loved airports and the sense of anticipation among bustling passengers. The aroma of freshly brewed coffee hung in the air, while agitated travelers waited for flights, wrestled with luggage, or attempted to sleep upright in padded chairs. Taking their cue, she settled into a chair next to Natasha, and closed her eyes for a few moments rest.

"Hey, no falling asleep." Natasha jabbed an elbow into Sara's side. "We only have twenty minutes until boarding, and I need your moral support."

"I'm so exhausted. The past week was completely draining." Sara opened her eyes and watched Natasha nervously fiddle with her passport. "Are you okay? I know you hate flying, but I thought you did really well on the last flight." She rolled up the sleeve of her sweater. "See, only a couple of nail marks."

Natasha gasped. "Sorry about that. Trust me, I'm better than I used to be. I think poor Beth is literally scarred for life after all the travelling we've done together over the years. For me, flying is just one of those fears, you know?"

"Oh, I know all about fears." Sara focused on several guys lurking at the gate, each one subtly peering over at the girls. She had to shake this constant fear of being followed.

"I hate to bring it up, Sara, but have you checked

your messages today?"

"Yes, I checked a few minutes ago when I phoned my Dad. There hasn't been anything at all since Monday, thank goodness."

"That's awesome. Maybe *The Eagle* finished playing his little game and will leave you alone at last."

Sara twirled a ringlet tightly around her finger. "I hope he hasn't moved on to some other poor girl. It's so cruel. I can't get the messages out of my head. I keep wondering if he's following us, which is ridiculous and irrational. I should be relieved he hasn't bothered me this week, and try to forget about the whole thing."

"Easier said than done?" Natasha's big blue eyes misted.

"I'm hopeless, aren't I? If it's not the fear of being followed, then there's also my fear of performing in front of large crowds, which is equally absurd, considering the path I'm taking. And then there's the fear of letting people down..."

Natasha shoved her passport inside her purse and turned to face Sara. "I get the first two, but what do you mean about having a fear of letting people down? I can't say that I've ever really considered it."

Bethany looked up from reading her book in the next seat along. "Nat, I think it has something to do with your different upbringing. Sara, I've noticed you always go out of your way to be kind—you go the extra mile, even if it's a hardship for you. Almost like you need to earn the approval of others. Am I right?"

Sara shrugged. "I guess so."

Natasha bristled. "So, you're saying that I'm not kind and never go out of my way for people? That's charming." She held her purse tightly on her lap and pouted.

"Oh, Nat, you know that's not what I mean. I love you like you were my own sister, for heaven's sake. But you have to see that you and I had a pretty privileged upbringing, and a sense of entitlement often comes with the package. We never thought twice about others doing things for us, and if we are totally honest, we were a little selfish. We didn't particularly care if we let others down. But I think we've both changed."

"A lot." Natasha grabbed Sara's hand. "But you mustn't worry about letting us down. You know that, right? And you shouldn't let the fear of disappointing others force you into doing things you don't want to do. I'm already feeling super guilty about getting you into this music business."

Sara shook her head. "No, you've got it wrong. I'll always be grateful to you and your family for opening the doors for me to follow my dream. I wonder sometimes if maybe it happened a little earlier than I would have chosen, like finishing high school first would have been better, but I realize you have to take the opportunity when it comes. God is in control, and I trust His timing." She looked down at her new leather boots and touched her stylish wool jacket. "My life has changed more than you'll ever know."

Bethany rose from her chair, set her book down, and crouched in front of Sara. "This has been quite the year. All of us have changed in different ways. And we'll go on changing throughout our lives. Teen years are pivotal—that's what Aunt Alice says. We have a lot going on. When I went through a really rough patch after my parents' accident, even after I turned to God, I struggled with being afraid. I was fearful that I would never dance again, and that Aunt Alice would be taken from me in some freak accident. I was even afraid Steve would steal her away and I'd be left all alone. She wrote out a Bible verse in her beautiful calligraphy, and now I have it framed on my bedside table."

"Oh, I totally know the one you mean." Natasha dug inside her coat pocket. "She even wrote it out for me and tucked it in my pocket before the first flight. Here it is. Psalm fifty-six, and verse three. It says: 'When I am afraid, I put my trust in You.'"

"Sounds pretty simple." Sara sighed and closed her eyes again.

"Yeah," Bethany agreed. "But God doesn't expect us to always get it the first time. I know I can be stubborn. But at the end of the day, God is completely trustworthy, and I can't imagine being in safer hands."

"This conversation sounds deep." Alice arrived with an array of snacks to tide them over for the rest of the journey. "Is everyone alright?"

Sara nodded. "Better, thanks. You guys are the best, you know that, right?"

"Duh. Of course we do." Natasha flashed a super white smile and stuffed the note back in her pocket. "Come on, ladies. We have a plane to catch. And one of you lucky ducks gets to sit next to me."

"I am so done with flying and I am absolutely freezing to death." Natasha huddled in the corner of a brightly colored sofa, and refused to take off her coat. "I'm sleeping in my coat, too. Can someone please crank up the heat?"

Sara's gaze darted around the rustic cabin-style suite, and she decided she loved the picturesque Big White resort. Two red, overstuffed armchairs flanked a stone fireplace, and identical sofas covered in plaid throws faced the fire. She walked over and covered Natasha with one of the throws.

"There you go, Princess."

"Thanks. You are a gem."

While Alice checked out the cupboards in the tiny kitchen, Sara opened the door to the bedroom. Two queen-size comfortable-looking beds took up half the room, and another fireplace was situated in the corner. When she pulled open the floor-to-ceiling curtains, the view took her breath away.

"You guys, you have to come and see this!"

All four of them gathered at the full wall of windows, and gazed at the night scene before them. The adorable little village below was alive with evening strollers and night skiers, and each tree was lit with fairy lights, some even laden with Christmas ornaments. Inviting storefronts and restaurants beckoned passersby, and the whole scene looked like a magical Christmas card in the ambient lamp-light.

"Wow." Alice put her arms around the girls in her care. "I think we are going to like it here. If I wasn't so utterly exhausted, I'd suggest checking it all out."

Bethany yawned. "It'll still be there tomorrow. I'm bushed. First dibs on the bathroom."

Natasha slid open the French windows, which caused a burst of cold air with a hint of wood smoke to blow into the room. She let out a deafening cheer.

"Nat, what on earth are you doing? It's already chilly in here and I thought you were freezing to death." Bethany bent down and switched on the electric fireplace, which instantly *swooshed* to life.

Natasha turned around and grinned. "I found a way to warm up, girls. There's a hot tub right on our balcony. Who's coming in?"

"Not me." Bethany ran into the bathroom, and Alice was already in her pajamas.

Sara shrugged. "I don't think I could sleep quite yet. I'll come out there with you. I've never been in a hot tub before."

"Really?" Natasha's face contorted, and then broke into a smile. "Oh, in that case you simply have to come. Let's change into swimsuits. Be fast—this is going to be painfully cold until the bliss soaks in."

Sara grinned and felt ten years old again. In rapid

time they changed, located the controls on the deck, found towels, and persuaded the lid of the hot tub to fold down. Sara's teeth chattered uncontrollably, and her hair felt almost solid on her head.

"Here, use this." Natasha took an extra hair tie from her wrist, and passed it to Sara. Both girls piled their masses of hair up in buns on top of their heads, before stepping into the hot water. Natasha gracefully sank into the bubbles, while Sara half-fell and landed with an ungainly splash.

Natasha smiled. "Smooth."

"Oh my, I thought soaking in the claw-footed tub at your house was luxurious." Sara sighed. "This is unreal." She sank into the whirling water until her shoulders were completely submerged, and only her head was above the surface. Natasha's eyes closed, and she was apparently warm for the first time in hours. The faint sounds from the village drifted on the night air, and when Sara looked up into the inky sky, she gasped.

"Natasha, look up there. Did you ever see so many stars in the sky? It's magnificent."

"Hmm. I love it when God does that."

"What?"

"Gives us a glimpse of how powerful and big He truly is. He's quite the Creator."

Sara marveled at the sheer magnitude of His grandeur. "This is unbelievable. I wish I could stay here and drink this sight in forever."

"Yeah, I know what you mean. Helps all your other worries fly away, doesn't it?"

For the first time in days, Sara truly relaxed. Fears, stress, anxiety, and the agenda for the next few days all dissipated, as if melting in the warm bubbles around her. She was loved by the Creator of all this. She soaked in that truth.

"Look, Sara. Snowflakes are falling."

Sara laughed when frozen specks danced on her face and landed on her lips and eyelashes. She opened her mouth and caught some on her tongue. She never felt more content and alive.

"Crazy how you can feel invigorated by the cold and soothed by the heat all at the same time, don't you think, Natasha?"

"Crazy good."

"Yeah. I'll never forget this moment."

Natasha pointed her toes out of the water, and quickly pulled them in again. "I want to stay in here all night. I don't think I was made for the cold. Sunrises and beaches are more my thing. But maybe snow will be yours, Sara. It's good to see you finally relaxed after all the drama recently."

"I know. We were meant to come on this trip, that's for sure. No cyber-stalker is going to stop me from following my dream." She closed her eyes and basked in the knowledge that she was in God's hands.

Sara smiled and whispered into the black night, "When I am afraid, I put my trust in You."

~ *Nine* ~

*S*ara woke the next morning to the unmistakable aroma of bacon and eggs. Delicious. She stretched on her side of the bed, careful not to disturb Natasha, who slept soundly in the space next to her. Sara glanced at the other bed, and knew Bethany and Alice were the chefs responsible for breakfast, which wafted enticingly from the kitchen. She pulled a sweater over her fleece pajamas, and popped into the bathroom before making her way to the little eating area.

"Hi, Sara. How did you sleep?" Alice wiped the counters down and smiled. Even first thing in the morning, she looked effortlessly beautiful.

"Like a log. Only a couple of elbows from Natasha, but I think the soak in the hot tub really helped me relax. I see you're the head cook, Bethany."

Bethany turned from the oven with a spatula in her hand. "Aunt Alice is improving in the kitchen for sure, but we thought it might be safer for me to take charge of the cooked breakfast. It'll warm us up before we head out for the day."

Sara found the cutlery drawer. "Shall I set the table?"

"Sure, thanks. I guess I should go and wake sleeping beauty." Alice took a deep breath and disappeared into the bedroom.

"Rather her than me." Bethany grimaced. "Natasha's not exactly a morning person. So are you ready for some snowshoeing today? It's so much fun, and it's a great way to see the mountain."

Sara shrugged and poured coffee into four chunky mugs. "I'll give it a go. I've never done anything like this

69

before, and from what I've read, it seems a lot less intense than skiing."

"Yeah, it's quite straightforward. Plus, it's a fantastic workout. Nat and I tried it once in Aspen a few years ago. My dad loved it." Bethany's eyes pooled and she brushed her cheek with the back of her hand.

"It doesn't get any easier, does it?" Sara leaned against the table. Her heart broke for her friend's enormous loss. "Two years seem to have flown by since the accident, but I know it's still painful for you."

Bethany flipped the bacon onto a plate. "It's the hardest when I visit somewhere new. I still want to share experiences with my parents, you know? And I can't help reminisce about all the wonderful times I had with them growing up."

"Of course, and it's important you remember." Sara went to her friend and hugged her, and then quietly finished getting everything organized on the breakfast table.

"I'm starving." Natasha appeared, bleary-eyed but very put-together in her satin pajamas and fur slipper boots. "Must be the mountain air."

The four of them sat around the log table and dug into a hearty feast of fried eggs, bacon, toast, and coffee.

"That was scrumptious." Sara wiped her mouth with a napkin. "Great job, cooks."

Natasha stood and stretched. "Man, I need to work that off this morning. Thank goodness we're hitting the snowshoe trails. I fancy a hot shower to warm me up before we go."

Sara picked up her plate and walked over to the sink. "Natasha, why don't we quickly do these dishes? Alice and Bethany got up super early to make it for us, after all."

Natasha placed one hand on her hip. "Fine. I guess you can go and take your turns in the bathroom first."

Alice grabbed her phone from the armchair. "I'll quickly call Steve. You go ahead, Bethany."

"Thanks, girls." Bethany winked at Sara, and headed for the shower.

~ * ~

"Oh my, this is so much fun." Sara put one snow-shoe-clad foot in front of the other, and followed Bethany. "Although I don't think I look very cool with my technique."

Alice chuckled from behind her. "My main aim is to stay upright. You're doing great, girls, keep up the pace."

"I think we're the only ones on this trail," Bethany called back. "Look at this fresh powdery snow and all these giant Christmas trees. Isn't it the most gorgeous scene ever? It feels like we're in Narnia."

Natasha grunted. "I'm freezing."

"You'll soon warm up, Nat. Especially when we go up that hill ahead of us. You'll be peeling off the layers by the time we reach the top."

Sara groaned. This was harder than it looked. "Do we really have to go up there? We're not all trained ballerinas who work out for hours each day, you know."

"What about me?" Alice laughed. "I'm not a ballerina or a teenager. We can do it. It'll be fun."

The chatter died down while they concentrated on the hike. Sara soon got used to the strange, stumpy skis on her feet, and apart from stepping on her own shoes a few times, she felt pretty good with her efforts.

It truly was a stunning resort. Behind them, colorful townhouses and rustic lodges dotted the picturesque village, and before them lay the natural beauty of snow-covered mountains. Sara inhaled through her nose, enjoying the pure, clean mountain air. It was chilly and crisp, but felt so good. Her cheeks stung with the bite of cold, but thanks to Natasha's spare ski clothes she borrowed, the rest of her felt warm enough. The only sounds she heard were the padding of their footsteps on snow. Everything else was muffled and silenced by the blanket of white. It was almost eerie. No, she wouldn't go there.

When they neared the top of the steep hill, Sara was at the back of their group, and for some reason, every few steps she was compelled to look behind her.

Just because I hear a snapping twig, it doesn't mean the stalker or some other creep is following me. Get a grip, Sara.

Breathing was hard work, and far from natural. Whooshing in her ears caused a sense of panic to bubble from the pit of her stomach.

"Are you okay back there, Sara?" Natasha shouted into the silence. She turned briefly to make sure. "You're heavy-breathing like crazy and it's freaking me out here."

Sara gave the thumbs up and hoped her dark sunglasses hid the fear in her eyes.

Why now? Why does every tree look like it's harboring a shadowy figure? Is it my insane imagination or is someone following me? Why can't I get this fear out of my head and enjoy this beautiful place? Think, think... When I am afraid, I put my trust in You.

"Okay girls, we made it. Let's take a water break." Alice pulled her bottle out of her small pack and guzzled half the contents. "I really hope that was the hardest part. I have a photo shoot to do this afternoon, and I'm going to be passed out at this rate."

"Are you sure you're all right, Sara?" Bethany stopped drinking. "You don't look so good."

Sara nodded as she bent over at the waist, and tried to catch her breath and calm her pounding heart.

"Hey, ladies." A loud, obnoxious male voice nearly caused Sara to go into cardiac arrest. She popped her head up and saw a group of three guys snowshoeing toward them. They looked like they were in their twenties at least, and were slowing down as if they wanted to chat.

Sara panicked. "Let's go." Without even attempting to take a swig from her water bottle, she passed the surprised men, refused to even acknowledge them, and led the way for the other girls to follow.

One of the guys muttered, "Uptight," and Sara heard Natasha apologize profusely while she followed the trail. When they were out of earshot of the men, Alice caught up with Sara.

"What is it? You seem awfully jumpy, Sara. It's not like you at all. Are you nervous out here on the mountain?"

Sara slowed her pace so she could answer. "I'm sorry. That was rude of me. But I can't help picturing my stalker behind every tree we pass. How pathetic is that? I know it's illogical, but this *Eagle* guy seems to have really messed with my head, and I can't forget about him."

"Did you get another message this morning?"

"No. I didn't even check. I didn't want to ruin the day. But I think I will take a look when we get back to our room."

"Good idea. It'll put your mind at rest. So, how about we conquer this mountain trail? I'm already thinking about the hot chocolate with whipped cream we'll get at the restaurant as our reward."

Sara grinned. "Now that sounds like an incentive. And you're right—I'm allowing my overactive imagination to get the better of me today. There are enough people on the trail now to make it feel safe, and who knows if I'll ever get an opportunity like this again. Thanks Alice, you always make me feel better."

"No problem. Now, let's show the ballerinas how it's done."

~ * ~

"You guys are amazing. I can't believe how glamorous I look, thanks to your handiwork."

Sara stared at her reflection in the full-length bathroom mirror. She had to admit, the soft blue sweater was perfect with the white skinny jeans. Black leather ankle boots and Bethany's faux fur jacket would complete the

73

ensemble for outdoor shots. Alice tamed Sara's unruly long curls into perfect glossy ringlets, and Natasha expertly applied stage make-up to accentuate her bright turquoise eyes.

"You should make this effort every day." Natasha grinned, clearly satisfied with her work. "I can teach you how to create this dramatic look, you know."

Sara wrinkled her nose. "Do you really think this is me? I prefer zero make-up and a ponytail."

Natasha huffed.

"You look stunning." Bethany held both of Sara's hands. "But you always do. Beautiful from the inside out."

Sara felt her cheeks heat up. "Thanks."

"Okay." Alice glanced around at her photography equipment. "I think I have everything we need." She clapped her hands. "Ready for your photo shoot, Miss Dean?"

Sara's stomach churned. "Let's get this over with. I apologize in advance for being the most unnatural model you've ever had the misfortune to photograph."

"Nonsense." Natasha struck a pose. "Pretend Alice is taking some snaps to send home to your family or something. Like vacation pictures. Try not to think about the posters and CD covers and the fact that your face will be plastered all over the Internet—"

"Nat. Really?" Bethany shook her head.

"What?" Natasha shrugged.

"Oh, no." Sara's shoulders froze. "The Internet. I completely forgot. I was going to check to see if I had any new messages from *The Eagle*. I was so carried away with you guys doing my makeover, it completely slipped my mind."

Alice stopped Sara in her tracks. "That's a good thing, sweetie. It means he isn't constantly consuming your thoughts. Hopefully, this will blow over and you can get back to concentrating on your singing."

Sara exhaled. "I need to check. I won't be able to relax now until I do. Is that okay? I'll be super quick."

"Go ahead. Otherwise I know it'll be on your mind all afternoon." Alice passed the laptop to Sara, and they all piled on the bed while the Internet loaded.

Natasha drummed her fingers on the bedside table. "This is painfully slow."

"We are up in a mountain resort, Nat." Bethany leaned against her. "I guess we're lucky to have any connection at all. Oh wait, here it goes."

Sara's pulse quickened when she scrolled down her list of emails. On one, the subject line simply said: "Canada?"

She clicked onto the message, and read it aloud:
"Running away to Canada?
You can't escape The Eagle.
Eagles fly, too."

Sara felt like she might throw up. She shivered even though the bedroom was now heated like a furnace.

Alice pulled out her phone, and Sara overheard her relaying the message to Steve, presumably to pass on to his police friend. Natasha and Bethany squashed her between them in a group hug, careful not to disturb her polished look.

"Don't cry." Natasha furrowed her brow. "Please don't ruin your make-up."

"Nat!" Bethany threw her hands in the air.

"No, I'm serious." Natasha took hold of Sara's shoulders and looked her in the eye. "You listen to me. You are strong. You have your faith. This *Eagle* is a vindictive coward who wants to ruin your life, and it's up to you whether you let him or not. It wasn't a threat or even anything cruel. He's being a jerk reminding you he's keeping tabs on you. That's all. Sara, you can't let fear destroy you."

"Nat, why don't you leave her alone?" Bethany put an arm around Sara's rigid shoulders. "This is horrible."

"No." Sara's voice didn't sound quite right but she continued. "Natasha's got a good point. I dragged you all up here for this photo shoot, and you performed a miracle by making me look like a movie star. I might dissolve later on, but for now, I will not cry. No tears. Perfect make up. 'When I am afraid, I put my trust in You.' That's the verse I'm living by every single day." She felt a flood of relief and a surge of adrenalin course through her veins. "Let's go, Alice."

Alice stood with her mouth open. She slowly picked up her gear, as if any startling movement might spook Sara into changing her mind. "Are you sure? We can put it back an hour if you need some time. The light will be good for a while yet."

"Positive. Listen, I don't want to think about *The Eagle* knowing I'm in Canada, or the fact that he might be watching me, although the message doesn't state he is here. Just that he can fly." She shuddered. "I didn't broadcast the trip in school, but lots of kids knew I was doing a photo shoot and I guess anyone could easily find out where." She fanned her hands at her face, desperate to not let a tear drop. "Oh, I'm talking nonsense. I don't know what to think. It's probably a scare tactic, but I won't let it stop me."

Alice nodded. "Okay, but I'm going to have a discreet word with the security up here at the resort. I contacted them before we came and explained our little situation. They've been really sweet about checking in with me ever since we arrived."

"Really, Aunt Alice?" Bethany fussed with one of Sara's ringlets. "I'm impressed. We had no clue you did that."

"I didn't want to cause any unnecessary alarm, or make you all feel self-conscious. But now I'm glad I put them in the picture. They can keep an extra look out, just to make us feel better."

Natasha wrapped a scarf around her neck and located her boots. "We'll come, too. Think of us as your personal bodyguards. Right, Beth? That way, Sara, you can focus on Alice and not worry about anyone hanging around and freaking you out."

Sara broke into a smile. "Perfect. I get my very own ballerina bodyguards."

~ *Ten* ~

"*A*nd that's a wrap." Alice lowered her camera and briskly rubbed her hands together. "Well done, Sara, you were amazing. I'm sure we'll have a great portfolio of usable shots for Gracelight."

Sara shivered and stomped her boots in the snow. "Thank goodness. I can't believe how chilly it became once the sun disappeared. Are you okay?"

"Yeah, but my fingers are absolutely freezing, so why don't we hustle into the village center and meet the others in the restaurant? They're holding a table for us."

Sara bit her lip to hide the grin on her face. She knew Natasha had Alice's little surprise wrapped and ready at the restaurant. Her stomach gurgled on cue. "Oh, yes please. The mountain air gives me a ravenous appetite. And Alice, thank you so much for doing this."

Alice threw her gear bag over one shoulder and thrust her hands into a pair of woolen mittens. "It was my pleasure. And once you got into the swing of it, I think you quite enjoyed yourself. Am I right?"

They plodded down a quiet walkway in the village.

"Maybe 'enjoy' is a bit of a push, but it wasn't half as bad as I imagined. That's mainly because you put me at ease and got me to chat and eventually relax. Plus this is such a beautiful spot for a winter shoot. It's absolutely perfect."

"And I think it helped that Natasha and Bethany hung around, too. When they weren't making you laugh for the serious poses, that is."

Sara giggled. "Okay, maybe I did enjoy myself a little bit. I only hope Gracelight is pleased with the results.

I'd hate to disappoint them after all the trouble they went to."

"Hey, promise me?" Alice pleaded.

"Hmm?"

"Promise me you'll try to quit being so fearful of what you think everyone expects from you? If these photos aren't good enough, it will be down to me. Not you. You did exactly what I asked of you. So, if they are not quite what Gracelight has in mind, then we'll come up with another plan. You have to stop spiraling everything into a whirlwind of impending doom."

Sara nodded. "You're right. You know me too well. I wasn't like this a year ago, was I?"

They reached the restaurant, but stood under the gabled porch roof and continued their conversation.

"You've always had a sensitive side, Sara, that's one of your beautiful qualities. It draws people to you, even though you're shy. I remember how hard you took your grandmother's passing, and then when Bethany went through losing her parents, you were so tender, and said exactly the right thing to her."

Sara blinked back tears.

Alice smiled. "I'll bet you are holding back the tears right now because you don't want to disappoint Natasha the make-up artist. Anyway, I think you have taken on a lot more than you anticipated this year. It's been tough for you, sweetie, hasn't it?"

Sara nodded, allowing a tear to fall freely.

"Getting your singing contract, moving out of your home and in with Natasha, keeping your awesome grades at school, and dealing with all the usual teen stuff is more than most can handle. Let alone *The Eagle* problems. You bottle a lot up because you don't want to be a burden on anyone. You want a quiet life but you desire to be where God wants you. You end up being fearful of so much, it hurts."

79

Sara gasped. "Alice, how do you know all this? It's like you're in my head or something."

Alice's eyes pooled. "Because that was me when I was about your age. Minus the singing and the stalker. It was before my parents died, but they were missionaries abroad and my sister and I had to figure a lot of stuff out for ourselves back here in the States. She was confident and I pretty much lived in fear."

"I had no idea." Sara shivered. "How did you turn yourself around? Get over the fear and everything?"

"God had a message for me. I'd read it a hundred times before but one day it almost leaped from the pages of my Bible. It was my turning point. I'll copy it out and leave it with you this evening if you like. But we should get into the warm before we both freeze to death out here."

"Alice?"

"Yes?"

"Thanks for always being here for me." Sara felt warmer already, and they hadn't even stepped foot inside the restaurant.

~ * ~

"Sara, we're over here." Natasha's booming voice rose above the ambient noise in the cozy Italian restaurant. Sara scanned the room and saw Natasha sitting by Bethany at a table for four, next to a roaring fire.

"Perfect." She waved for Alice to follow her, and they wove around tables and servers to reach their destination. Garlic, spicy sauces, and something cheesy wafted on the air, and raucous laughter came from a group of older women by the window. Natasha winked at Sara—the signal to say the photo frame was stashed and ready to give to Alice.

Natasha gave a brief rundown of the best items on the menu, while Sara and Alice removed layers of outerwear and made themselves comfortable.

"This is awesome." Alice pulled her camera from her

bag and captured images of the three girls talking animatedly in front of the huge fireplace.

Bethany grabbed Sara's hand and gave it a squeeze. "You were fantastic this afternoon. I can't wait to see the shots where you threw snowballs and made a snow angel on the ground. And then when those giant snowflakes fell as if on cue, and they caught in your hair and on your eyelashes—it was completely magical."

"So glad I used waterproof mascara on you." Natasha checked her own reflection in her hand mirror, and popped it back in her purse. "Gracelight is going to love them all, I know it."

Sara was about to make a comment on how she wasn't so sure, and maybe she could have done better, but she caught Alice's eye, and instead she smiled and simply said, "Thanks. All of you."

Alice passed the camera to the girls. "Take a look at the one on the screen."

Natasha gasped. "Whoa. Sara, I know I can take credit for the painting on of the make-up, but those eyes are all natural beauty. Alice pulled out something special from you here." She tilted the camera so Sara could see clearly.

"Wow." A lump caught in Sara's throat. It was a close-up, and her bright turquoise eyes looked heavenward, with a snowflake perched majestically on her long, dark eyelashes. It was a precious split second, which captured pure joy from within, free from anxiety and stresses and pressures and fears. Simple joy. She grinned. "I think I need to keep this one close by to remind me how I should live my life."

Alice took the camera from her. "I'll have that one enlarged for you. It's perfect."

Natasha picked up a leather menu. "Okay, now how about some lasagna? I'm starving."

"Oh, that sounds delicious." Sara licked her lips.

"Listen girls, you have no idea how much this means to me—you all travelling here and being a huge part of my life. I have the best friends in the world."

"You certainly do." Natasha winked.

"And I know you probably don't know whether to bring up the elephant in the room or not..."

"What elephant?" Natasha whispered to Bethany.

"*The Eagle*," Bethany whispered back.

"Oh. *That* elephant."

"Anyway, I think we should spend this evening talking about other things. No conversations about eagles, stalkers, police or security. Agreed?"

"Whatever you prefer." Alice smiled. "You know, we are here when you want to unload but I think a fun evening is in order."

"Sounds good to me." Bethany lifted one eyebrow. "I'm guessing we might have to discuss fun things like a certain wedding that is fast approaching?"

Alice sighed. "I can hardly wait, you guys. And I couldn't have done all the planning without you. I know it's been a bit consuming but I am truly grateful for my beautiful bridesmaids."

Natasha lifted a silver package tied with pink ribbon from the depths of her purse and set it in front of Alice.

"Whatever is this?"

Bethany cleared her throat. "We knew you still had to decide what to use for your 'something borrowed' and 'something old', so Natasha's mom found an item we think will mean a great deal to you."

Natasha pushed it closer to Alice. "Go ahead, open it."

Sara watched Alice's face transform from wonder, to realization, then to joy. Tears meandered down all their faces, and for a moment nobody could speak. A waiter came to the table, observed their tears, and swiftly departed.

"Thank you all." Alice sniffled. "I haven't seen this photo before—it must have belonged to Anita, my sweet sister. It's beautiful. I do recognize the pearl frame, though." She turned to Bethany. "Your dad gave it to your mom one birthday. I remember Natasha's mom admired it so much, Anita promised she would display a photo of the two of them inside."

"Yes, originally there was a picture of my mother with Beth's mom in the frame." Natasha fanned her face. "Two best friends. Oh, this is too much."

"Aunt Alice, we arranged for the florist to entwine it somehow in your bridal bouquet, if that's what you would like. That way your family will be with you when you walk down the aisle."

"Oh, it's a wonderful idea." Alice gazed at the photo again and sighed. "Thank you all so much. I'm at a loss for words."

Sara raised a water glass. "In that case, would you all join me in a toast? To the stunning bride-to-be, to her three trusty bridesmaids, to family past and present, and to the greatest of friends. Cheers."

Glasses clinked and Sara's heart swelled.

~ Eleven ~

*A*ll the girls were up bright and early on Sunday morning. A taxi was due to collect them from the resort at nine, followed by a short flight to Vancouver. Sara noticed an envelope with Alice's intricate handwriting on top of her suitcase, but tucked it inside her purse to read later on, when she was feeling a little more awake.

Alice breezed into the living room. "Okay, I checked out, and I thanked the security guy for looking out for us. The taxi should be here any minute, so are we packed and ready to go?"

"How come I can't close my stupid case?"

Natasha wrestled with her zipper until Bethany came to her rescue and sat on top of the case.

"Do you think maybe it was the sweaters you bought in that darling store in the village?" Bethany asked with a grin.

Natasha huffed. "I had to buy a souvenir or three. I didn't think they would take up so much room." The zipper finally cooperated. "There we go. No problem."

Sara pulled on her jacket and wheeled her case to the door. "It's been fantastic. I'm going to miss this place."

Alice squeezed Sara's hand. "At least you have a portfolio full of photographs to remember it by. I made sure there were plenty of the mountains and the village, too. And I have a ton of the resort—after all, that was my original assignment for the magazine."

"I almost forgot about that." Bethany joined them with her luggage. "I guess you snapped away constantly without us even realizing."

"My camera feels like an extra limb sometimes but

this certainly is a stunning destination to photograph. I love my job. And I'm really looking forward to taking some shots at the concert tonight." Alice shivered. "Oh my goodness, I already have butterflies in my stomach for you girls. It's going to be spectacular. All my girls performing together."

Bethany grinned. "I can't wait. Doing my favorite thing alongside my favorite people is special."

"Aren't you nervous at all?" Sara asked. Her insides were flip-flopping already.

"We've practiced enough that I could do both routines in my sleep. Your songs are so beautiful it makes dancing feel natural and easy, compared to some of the performances we've done over the years. This is dancing for joy. Literally."

"Wow." Sara's throat dried up merely thinking about going on stage. "In that case, I'm going to sing for joy."

Natasha snorted. "Okay, let's get all this joy on the road." She slung her purse over one shoulder and wheeled her bulging case through the door. "Even though I detest the thought of being up in the air again so soon. Vancouver, here we come."

~ * ~

The flight was smooth and on time, which was a huge answer to prayer since their schedule was tight. Four hours after they landed at the Vancouver airport, Sara sat alone on a red vinyl sofa in the "green room" at one of the city's largest churches. She attempted to breathe slowly. Her hands were shaking uncontrollably and she felt nauseous.

A kindly older woman poked her head around the doorway. "Can I get you anything, Miss Dean?" Her name badge read: "Vera—how may I help you?"

Sara looked up. "Thank you, Vera, but I'm fine. I have enough water—actually I already spilled some down my blouse. And I can never eat anything before I sing, but maybe I'll nibble on some of these lovely snacks later. I really appreciate the thought."

Vera smiled. "I understand, dear. I'm on my way to collect your dancer friends from their room. I'll be praying for you. It's a sold out concert tonight, you know."

"That's what I heard. I'm afraid I can't take the credit for that. The other band is the main attraction."

Vera chuckled. "So humble. You might be young and new, dear, but my granddaughter is actually here to listen to you. They play your song on the Christian radio station all the time."

"Seriously?" Sara's pulse quickened. This was really happening.

"I told you so." A familiar voice came from behind Vera.

Sara did a double take. "Megan? I didn't know you would be here in person." She jumped up from the sofa and ran to her Gracelight manager. "It's so good to see you. You're just in time."

Vera smiled and scurried off down the corridor, leaving the two of them to talk.

Megan laughed. "I know. It was a bit last minute." She dumped her overnight bag in the corner, draped her purple coat across a chair, and headed straight to the coffee pot. "I managed to work in a couple of days' vacation so that I could visit my sister. She lives a couple of hours outside Vancouver, so it's perfect. You look stunning tonight. Did your friends do the make-over thing again?"

"Yes, they really are my angels. Natasha's an expert with stage make-up from all the ballet shows she's been in, and Bethany is used to taming curly hair with all of her long ringlets. Alice is about the same size as me, so she loaned me the black silk blouse, and Natasha insisted on buying these leather skinny jeans for me. She said her mom wanted to help in some way." She looked down at her outfit. "That family is beyond generous."

"And the look is absolutely perfect. It's young but

86

classy. I like it. Anyway, how have you been, Sara? How was the photo shoot?"

Glad for the distraction from her current bout of nerves, Sara gave details about the shots in the snow and their fun time at the resort.

"Sara, Alice filled me in about this stalker who's been giving you a hard time online. I'm really sorry. I know it's unnerving. Unfortunately, stuff like this happens more often when you are in the public eye. I'm relieved it's only on the Internet, but I can't imagine how frustrating it must be." She tipped Sara's chin up and looked at her intently. "Are you sure you're okay?"

Sara nodded. "It's not that serious, but it has freaked me out. You know how much I struggle with all the attention—good or bad. But Alice, Steve, and the girls have been fantastic."

"What about your family? Are they freaking out, too?" Megan screwed up her nose. "I know they're not exactly thrilled about this contract—they haven't been very supportive."

Sara chewed a fingernail and then realized she was nibbling on Bethany's manicure efforts. "They were worried when I told them, but they know I'm in good hands. They've got a lot on their plate right now. But I promised to keep them up to date. I'll go see them when I get home."

"And are you happy with the band tonight? They're a professional bunch of guys and they assured me they practiced your songs thoroughly. Was sound check okay?"

"Perfect. They're talented."

"So are you, my dear." Megan glanced at her watch. "It's almost time for you to go on. Are Bethany and Natasha all set to do their routines?"

Sara nodded. "They helped me get ready first but they should be at the stage any minute. That lady, Vera, was going to give them a last call in their room down the hallway. Thanks again for agreeing to let them be a part of this. They are amazingly talented dancers, and the two songs at the end of my set fit perfectly with their choreography."

"I'm looking forward to seeing the overall effect. I know they both have stellar reputations in the San Francisco dance world. Now, are you warmed up and everything?"

"Yes." She began pacing. "But my stomach is still in knots. I hoped my nerves wouldn't be as bad this time. Isn't it supposed to get easier with each concert?"

Megan chuckled. "For some. But being nervous isn't necessarily a bad thing. It makes us more reliant on God. You have four incredible numbers to get through, all with amazing words packed with hope and truth. He'll give you strength. And then you can enjoy the rest of the concert."

"You're right." Sara took a deep breath. "I think I'll head out and wait at the side of the stage. Will you be in the audience?"

"Oh, yes." Megan picked up her purse and coffee, and gave Sara a quick hug. "Alice is saving me a seat in the front row. Has to be some perks to this job. I'll be praying for you, Sara, and I'll come back here when it's all over. You'll be wonderful. Enjoy."

"Thanks. Will you tell Vera I will be out in two minutes, please?"

"No problem."

Sara knew she should get a move on but suddenly remembered the envelope Alice gave her at the resort first thing. For some reason, she had to read it right now. She opened her allocated locker and dug into her purse. Reverently, she unfolded the blush colored notepaper and read the contents out loud.

"'Do not be anxious about anything, but in every situation, by prayer and petition, with thanksgiving, present your requests to God. And the peace of God, which transcends all understanding, will guard your hearts and your minds in Christ Jesus.' Philippians 4:6-7."

Tears clouded her vision and she exhaled. When she folded the note back into her purse, she caught sight of the phone and had the urge to check for messages.

No, not now. God's peace is going to guard my heart and my mind.

Instead, she presented her requests to God, and followed the corridor to the stage.

Natasha and Bethany were already at the side of the curtain. They both turned when they heard her approach. Silently, they hugged Sara, and gave her hair and outfit one last primp.

"You two look like angels." She kept her voice a low whisper. Both girls wore their hair in long, soft curls, and had identical chiffon, flowing dance dresses in the palest peach color. "Thanks for being here with me."

Bethany's eyes brimmed with tears, and Natasha squeezed Sara's hand.

Vera stood behind them, and looked up from her clipboard with a smile. "I was about to come and find you, dear. The sound guys are ready and the emcee is about to head out on stage. Are you good to go?"

"Ready as I'll ever be." Sara sent up one last prayer for help and performed breathing exercises while she listened to her introduction by the emcee.

She put one foot in front of the other and gingerly walked onto the brightly lit stage, dreading she might trip. Immediately, that familiar peace she experienced only when she sang enveloped her like a hug. The crowd applauded loudly as the band played the first few bars, Sara smiled, picked up the microphone, and took her place in the spotlight.

~ *Twelve* ~

*S*ara felt emotionally and physically drained. She collapsed onto the sofa in the green room and closed her eyes.

Thanks, Lord. That was so amazing, and it was all because of You.

She savored the moment of peace and relative quiet until the frontline band started playing. She should at least go to the side stage and watch them perform, but the weekend's activities caught up with her all at once, and the idea of a power nap was incredibly appealing.

Bethany squealed and burst through the doorway "Sara, there you are. You were amazing." She flew across the room, plopped onto the couch, and gave her friend a tight hug. "Oh, my goodness, that was spectacular. Your voice had such an amazing quality to it, and they did a great job on sound. You looked so relaxed and confident up there. It blows my mind."

"It blows mine, too." Sara held up one hand horizontally, and it quivered. "This is the real me. Shaking like a leaf." She laughed. "God does a miracle every time I go on stage, you know."

"I know. That's what makes it so special. Nat and I had such a blast dancing along to your music. Thanks again for arranging all this."

"I loved having you up on stage with me. I can't wait to see Alice's photographs. She promised to take lots of you both dancing. Where's Natasha anyway?"

"She didn't want to miss any of the next band, so she headed straight out to our seats. I think she secretly has a major crush on the lead singer. Are you coming to watch the rest of the concert?"

Sara yawned. "I think I might stay here for a while.

Have a little rest. Then maybe I'll head over to the side stage and watch it from there. I don't want to miss too much of it, but I really feel done in. But you go on out and sit with Natasha."

"Are you sure?" Bethany's chocolate-brown eyes were like saucers. "I don't like the idea of you being all alone."

Sara smiled. "I do. How often do I get a little alone time these days? This is hard work for an introvert like me. Really, you go ahead and I'll see you after the show. And thanks for caring."

"You do look a little tired. I must admit, I can't wait to get on that plane later tonight and head home. It's been a long day."

"The longest." Sara stretched and closed her eyes. "See you later."

Bethany disappeared and the thud of music from the stage filled the room. The heavy bass resounded in Sara's chest, and she realized there was no way to escape the noise. "So much for taking a nap."

After five minutes, Sara stood and stretched, and then wandered over to the counter and picked on the grapes and cheese. Her stomach still felt a little unsettled, but it wasn't the nerves anymore. The phone beckoned from the locker, and she sighed before retrieving it from her purse.

Sara paced like a caged lion while waiting for numerous messages to load. There were a few from friends at church wishing her well at the concert, but nothing menacing. Her shoulders relaxed and she pocketed the phone. A sharp knock on the door made her jump. She caught her breath when a bouquet of white carnations appeared, followed by a gangly teenaged boy, who seemed even more embarrassed than Sara.

He thrust the flowers into Sara's arms, handed her a card, and mumbled, "Enjoy."

"Thanks." Sara racked her brain trying to think who might have sent the flowers. Maybe the Smithson-Blairs? They would definitely do something sweet like send flowers. Her parents certainly couldn't afford to splurge on something so frivolous.

She placed the flowers on the counter and ripped open the envelope. Her smile faded when she read the message:

"The mouse in concert? I hope you
lose your voice forever. The Eagle."

Sara grabbed the bouquet and thrust the whole thing into the garbage can.

"Why won't you leave me alone?"

She sobbed, and tucked the card safely inside her purse, ready to give to the police back in San Francisco. With no energy to pace, she slid down the wall and landed on the floor with a thump.

The phone vibrated in her pocket, and she pulled it out tentatively. Surely *The Eagle* wouldn't make contact?

It was her father.

Weird, he never phones.

Sara dabbed at her eyes with her sleeve and put on a brave voice. "Hi Dad." She sprang to her feet and closed the door, muffling some of the stage music.

"Sara, thank goodness." He sounded frantic—not his usual self at all.

"Dad, what is it?" She plugged a finger into her other ear to block out the noise.

"I'm sorry to call when you're busy with your concert, sweetheart but it's James. He ran away from home."

Silence followed while Sara processed the information. "What... James? How long has he been gone?"

"We're not exactly sure."

"How can you not be sure? What's going on, Dad?" Sara's heart beat a wild rhythm and she had to concentrate hard to make sure she heard everything correctly.

"You know how he's been lately—moody and hanging out with those tough guys across the street. Your mom went into his bedroom this morning because he didn't come down for breakfast, and his bed hadn't been slept in. We don't know if he was around last night at all. No one saw him after supper but that's nothing new. He often stays in his room playing music."

"But he could have been abducted, or in an accident or something. How do you know he ran away from home, Dad?"

"His backpack is missing, along with his winter coat, his wallet, and a box of cookies. Plus, he left a note."

Sara's breath caught in her throat. "A note? What did it say?"

"I have it right here. It says, *'I'm running away. I am sorry. James.'*"

"Oh, no. Poor boy." Sara sank back down to the floor. "He could be anywhere. Did he have much cash?"

"I wasn't aware that he had any. He spends whatever allowance we give him. Sara, do have any ideas where he might hide out?"

She raked her hand through her curls and shrugged. "I'm not sure. He's got a new set of friends since I was living at home. You could call his old friends, Simon and Marcus. They live just a few doors down. Maybe they've seen him?"

She heard an exasperated sigh. "Already tried them. They know nothing. I've been wandering downtown and at that park where he plays soccer sometimes, but it's like looking for a needle in a haystack."

"Is Mom there?"

"She is but she's not doing so well." Sara heard whispering in the background. "She can't come to the phone at the moment."

Sara slumped. "Have you reported James missing to the police?"

"Yes. Not that they can do much about a runaway. Your mom phoned them right away of course. She's a wreck. And the boys are worried, too—they're both quiet as mice here."

Sara shuddered at the word 'mice', but tried to focus. "Listen Dad, this concert will finish in an hour or so. My plane leaves late tonight, so I should be back in San Francisco in the morning. I'll come straight to the house. Will you promise to call or text if there's any news? I'll check in with you as soon as I land. I'll get there as soon as I can."

"I promise."

"If you need anyone there with you, I know Pastor Steve will come over. I'll text you his phone number, and get Alice to call him and fill him in. His friend, Jed, at the police station, might be able to help, too. It's worth a try, right?"

"Thanks, sweetheart. Sorry to burden you with this right now. I know it was a special night for you. I hope your concert went well. Your mom wanted to wait until tomorrow to tell you, but I knew you would want to know, and I thought you might have some ideas where we might look. Hey, you probably have some people who will pray or something, right?"

Sara blinked back tears. "Of course. I'll get our church praying. We have to believe James is safe. Maybe he'll show up at home tonight. It's awfully cold, isn't it?"

"Yes. Yes, it's awfully cold. But your brother is resourceful."

Sara exhaled slowly. "You're right. I have some calls to make, but stay in touch, okay, Dad?"

"I will. Love you, Sara."

"I love you, too."

With all thoughts of her own fears and insecurities swept aside, Sara prayed in earnest for her little brother.

She sent Steve's cell number to her father, and then

texted Alice, Natasha and Bethany. She explained a family emergency had come up, and that she needed to grab a taxi to the airport, in the hope of getting an earlier flight on standby.

Her limbs felt like she was wading through toffee as she collected all her belongings. Suddenly, the door swung open, and Alice, Natasha, Bethany, and Megan all rushed into the room.

"What's wrong?" Alice's face was ashen.

"It's James. He ran away from home, and my parents are frantic." Sara bit her lip. "And it's really cold. He's all skin and bones as it is." She glanced at the garbage. "And *The Eagle* sent me flowers."

Natasha grabbed Sara's bag. "What on earth? We need to get you home. You've been worried about James for a while, haven't you?"

"Yes." Sara sniffled. "I'm praying he's safe."

Megan observed the crushed flowers and took control of the situation. "Okay, you ladies need to go. There are always cabs right outside the entrance, and the concert is still going strong so it'll be quiet out there. Do you have all your luggage?"

Bethany opened a side door. "It's all right here. Do you think we'll get a standby flight?"

Megan pursed her lips. "Who knows? You might not all get on together. I suggest you let Sara take it alone if necessary. I'll square up everything here. Just go."

"Thanks so much, Megan. I'm sorry to leave in such a hurry." Sara slung her purse over her shoulder. This was such a disaster. "Will you thank the organizers for me? And apologize for me not sticking around to chat with the audience."

"Yes, they'll understand. Keep me informed, okay?"

Alice hugged Megan on her way passed, and promised to text later.

~ * ~

Sara and the others were transported to the airport with minimal fuss, and miraculously, Alice and Sara snagged the last two seats on an earlier flight. Exhausted and preoccupied, they travelled in silence and were both relieved when they finally landed in San Francisco. The luggage carousel took forever to spew out their cases, but by one in the morning, they were ready to leave the airport.

"There's Steve." Alice waved madly at the sight of her fiancé.

He jogged to meet them, and gave Alice a warm hug. He turned to Sara and gave her one, too. "It's going to be okay."

Sara nodded into his shoulder and took a shaky breath. "Did my dad phone you? Have you heard anything?"

Steve took a rolling case from each of them and started walking. "No, no news yet. I called your parents as soon as Alice texted me, and they said they were doing fine and didn't need me to go over there. I promised to set the prayer chain in motion with the church members, and said I'd drop you over at their house as soon as possible. Maybe they'll let me come in and wait with them?"

Sara shrugged. "Don't be offended by whatever they say. My mom is particularly anti-church these days. But you never know, they might appreciate the support. Alice, can we take you home on the way? You must be ready to drop by now."

Alice put an arm around Sara's waist as they trotted along to keep up with Steve. "I'm fine. And if it's okay with you, I'll tag along. I'll do whatever I can to help—make fliers, keep coffee coming, pray. I have to get used to being a pastor's wife soon anyway. Right, honey?"

Steve grinned. "You bet. You're going to be amazing."

They found Steve's minivan, loaded the luggage inside, and Sara checked in with her dad on the ride home.

"Nothing new?" Alice turned from the front passenger seat and faced Sara.

"No. I think it's going to be a long night. I wish James would come home. What could be so horrific to cause him to run away in the middle of winter? He seemed morose and maybe even a bit secretive last week when I visited, but I had no idea he was having any major issues. If only I'd insisted on spending some time with him. He may have opened up and I could have helped."

Sara sniffled and Alice passed her a Kleenex™.

Steve looked at Sara in the rearview mirror.

"Sometimes there's no warning." He took a ragged breath. "I've been working with kids and teens for long enough to know they can be unpredictable. They're able to bury a lot of pain under a guise of indifference or a bad attitude, and it's not easy to penetrate the walls they put up. James might have been hurting for a long time, or maybe something set him off and he acted on impulse. Whatever the reason, please don't beat yourself up."

"But he's my little brother and we used to be so close. I feel like maybe I abandoned him when I moved to Natasha's. I left him in a pretty stressful home. You know how my mom can be."

Alice reached a hand out. "You're a wonderful daughter and the most caring sister I could ever imagine. Right now we have to think of James and his well-being. All the other stuff can be discussed later, but everyone's priority has to be getting him home again. Don't let anyone try to make you feel guilty, okay? You've got nothing to feel guilty about. Be there for your parents and your little brothers, and pray."

"You're right. I have those Bible verses you gave me this morning. I thought they meant a lot when I was nervous before the concert, and then thinking about *The Eagle*, but they are even more special now. Prayer and peace. That's how I'm going to get through this. Oh, by the way Steve, *The Eagle* sent flowers to me at the concert."

"What?"

"It doesn't seem very important now. He knew I was singing there somehow and probably wanted to freak me out. I don't know. I was so mad I trashed the flowers but kept the card in case it held a clue."

"Good thinking. I'll let Jed know at the police station." Steve shook his head. "They may be able to trace payment for it or something. But you're right. Tonight our priority is James. And Sara?"

"Yes?"

"In spite of what you may think, you are one very courageous young lady."

~ Thirteen ~

"*S*ara, you're really here." Little Timothy wrapped his arms around his sister's hips and clung to her for dear life. "James is missing."

"Hey, Tim. Yes, I know about that. Are you doing okay?"

She felt him nod against her, and then a quiet sob escaped. "Jake is fast asleep, but I can't close my eyes."

"Oh, come here." Sara scooped her brother up in her arms and carried him into the living room.

"Sara, you must be exhausted, sweetheart." Mr. Dean hobbled over from the window and put a protective arm around her. "I'm sorry about all this. Did Alice come with you?"

"Yes, she's right behind me. Steve's with her, too. They really want to help out. I hope that's okay." A floorboard creaked and Sara looked over to the kitchen. Her mother leaned against the doorframe. Somehow she looked ten years older than she did last week. She was huddled in an oversized cardigan and sweatpants, and her eyes were red and swollen.

"Mom?" Sara handed Timothy to her father and rushed over to hug her mom. It was like embracing a plank of wood, but it made Sara feel a little better. "How are you holding up, Mom? Can I get you some tea or something to eat maybe?"

Mrs. Dean stared straight ahead, completely motionless. "I just want James home."

"Of course you do. We all do. Come and sit." Sara literally dragged her mother into the living room and lowered her onto the armchair. Alice and Steve quietly entered and closed the front door behind them. Steve shook

Mr. Dean's hand, and Alice stood next to Sara, and gave Mrs. Dean's shoulder a gentle squeeze.

Steve stuffed his hands in his pockets and shrugged. "I know this is a difficult night for you all, and Alice and I will leave if you want us to, but I think at times like this a family needs all the support it can get. We want to do whatever we
can to help."

Mr. Dean looked up. "We appreciate that."

Steve continued. "Can I ask what has been done already? And then perhaps we can figure out if there's anything productive we can do tonight. I realize it's very late but I'm happy to search an area, and I know I can call several others from church who will come out to help us."

"At this hour?" Mr. Dean shook his head. "It's almost two in the morning. We can't expect strangers to be out wandering the streets in the cold. They don't even know us."

"They would be more than willing." Alice perched on the edge of the sofa. "We have a team at church who are available to assist in such an emergency, day or night. They do it out of love. Which areas have been covered so far?"

Mr. Dean set Timothy on the floor, and the little boy staggered over to Sara for a cuddle.

"I went to all three parks in the immediate area. They are familiar to James, so I thought he might hang out there. And then our neighbors hunted around the mall for a couple of hours this afternoon, in case he tried to get warm inside."

"He must be freezing." Mrs. Dean rubbed her arms and pulled her cardigan tighter across her skinny frame. "It's cold enough to snow out there."

Sara knelt on the floor next to the armchair and pulled Timothy onto her lap.

"What about your neighborhood?" Steve asked. "Has anyone gone door-to-door? Perhaps some of the kids saw

James leave, or heard him mention something to give us some clues."

"I've spoken to everyone." Mrs. Dean's eyes transformed from glazed to furious, and her voice became shrill. "Don't you think I've tried everything I can think of? Don't you think I've grilled his friends and interrogated his brothers? Do you think I'm such a bad mother? Do you think he ran away because we're bad parents, just because we don't go to your perfect church?"

She stalked back into the kitchen, leaving an awkward silence in her wake.

Mr. Dean coughed loudly. "Sorry... nothing personal. It's been a tough day. It brought back the pain of when we lost our baby boy a few years ago. My wife can't bear the thought of losing another child."

"Poor Mom. I'll go and sit with her." Sara stood and stretched her aching limbs. "Alice, could you put Timothy to bed? Is that okay with you, Tim?"

The little boy nodded and picked up a ratty-looking blanket from the floor. "Come on, Alice. I think my eyes are ready to close now."

Alice winked at Sara and followed him along the narrow hallway.

The men decided to make some calls and then take a drive downtown. Steve was familiar with many of the popular hangouts for street kids, and Mr. Dean was grateful to do something practical.

Sara felt the chill of the night blow through the house when they left through the front door. She carried empty mugs into the kitchen and dumped them in the sink. Silence enveloped the room as she sat at the little kitchen table next to her mother.

"Mom, none of this is your fault. And nobody thinks you are a bad mother. My church is so far from perfect you wouldn't believe it, and Steve only wants to help. It's what he does. He's passionate about kids, and he's rescued several from life on the streets. Please don't be mad."

Mrs. Dean's elbows were on the table, and her hands supported her head. Her graying curly hair was tied in a ponytail and Sara had the sudden urge to do something she hadn't done in years. Without saying a word, she got up, opened the junk drawer under the counter, and dug out a hairbrush with pink roses on the handle. Standing behind her mother, Sara very gently eased the hair tie from her graying curls. When the hair fell freely, Mrs. Dean flinched, and then lowered her hands to her lap.

"I used to love doing this when I was young, Mom." Sara slowly brushed her mother's hair from root to tip in a therapeutic motion. "Your hair was even longer back then, and I thought you were like a princess with your golden curls."

"Not much gold left now."

"That doesn't matter. It's still beautiful. You are still beautiful."

Sara sensed her mother softly crying but continued brushing for several minutes. Time seemed to stand still. Sara closed her eyes. She could remember the joy she felt all those years ago in this very kitchen, simply spending time with her mother. The cherished girly moments when they shooed the males from the kitchen while they baked or read or brushed each other's hair. It was an eternity ago. How had they become so distant?

"Sara, I'm sorry."

The words were a mere whisper, and Sara's hand froze mid-stroke. She hadn't heard her mother speak in such a tender voice since the death of her baby brother. The day everything changed for their family.

"Mom, you don't have anything to be sorry for. You're understandably upset. We all are."

"No. I'm sorry for the years we've missed. You and I—you're my only daughter. I had a lot of time to think today, while I've been worrying about James. I was so scared of losing another child, then I realized I've already lost you."

Sara pulled the chair around and knelt in front of it, desperate to get a glimpse of the softness that used to glow from her mother's turquoise eyes. The turquoise eyes she inherited. It was there, clouded with tears, but the kindness hovered just below the surface. If only she could break through.

"Mom, you haven't lost me, and I'm sorry if you think I left you. Moving out seemed like the right thing to do for my singing career, and maybe we didn't communicate well enough, but I really thought you didn't mind."

"Didn't care, you mean. Oh Sara, I'm so foolish. I guarded my heart because I couldn't handle any more pain after losing the baby, and as a result I pushed you all away and made everyone miserable. Including myself." She looked down at her hands, worn and rough from years of cleaning jobs. "And now James has gone, too."

"No. Mom, I know you love us, and you always worked hard to care for us. It's been difficult, but I got through it all with my faith, with Jesus. Losing a brother, and then Grandma, and feeling so isolated and lonely most of the time was devastating to me. But everything changed. You remember? I couldn't stop telling you about God all the time."

A slight smile curled Mrs. Dean's mouth. "I remember I told you never to talk about church stuff in my house. You nearly drove us mad. But I know it helped you."

"It didn't make all the bad stuff go away but it gave me hope. It can give you hope, too, Mom."

Mrs. Dean reached out and touched Sara's face. "You are beautiful. Did I ever tell you that?"

Sara shook her head. Tears burned her eyes.

"I've missed so much. Maybe it took a night like this to wake me up. Come here."

Mother and daughter embraced for the first time in

years. Neither wanted to let go as they sobbed for lost time. And for the lost young boy somewhere out on the streets of San Francisco.

~ Fourteen ~

*E*arly morning light filtered through the horizontal, plastic blinds, and Sara curled up in a ball on the armchair. Her back ached and her head pounded. None of them slept a wink, except her little brothers, and now a new day arrived with still no word from James.

"Coffee?" Alice held two steaming mugs, and gave one to Sara and the other to Mrs. Dean, who lay huddled on the sofa. Steve made toast in the kitchen while Mr. Dean took a quick hot shower to warm up after spending the past several hours searching the streets for James.

"Thanks, Alice." Sara mustered a smile. "Does Steve have a cup? He must be freezing."

"I'm fine," Steve called from the kitchen. "But I'm hungry. I'll bring in a plate of toast and you can all eat to keep your strength up. I got a bag of doughnuts, too. I thought at least Jake and Tim would like them."

Mrs. Dean straightened. "Thank you, Steve. I think I'll start phoning around some of James' friends again. They should all be up getting ready for school. Maybe someone's heard something."

"James might have ended up at a buddy's house to crash for the night." Alice shrugged. "Steve's friend at the police station finished his shift and promised to stop by soon. He might have some ideas. I know it's tricky with a runaway—they can't exactly mount a full scale search, but we will certainly do everything we can."

Sara reached across the sofa and held her mom's hand. "I think James will come home on his own. He may need to blow off some steam. He's a smart boy, Mom."

Mrs. Dean nodded and blew her nose. She looked physically and emotionally drained.

The doorbell chimed, and Mrs. Dean jumped up and

rushed to answer it, closely followed by Sara. It was a police officer, and Sara gasped at the thought of him bearing bad news. She put an arm around her mother and braced herself.

"Hello, Mrs. Dean? I'm Jed, a friend of Pastor Steve. Sorry if I alarmed you. I just finished my shift, and decided to come straight over and see if there was anything I could help with. Also, I have some information for Sara Dean. Is that you, Miss?"

Sara nodded and collected herself. "Yes, please come on in."

The tall officer dwarfed the living room even more. He nodded to everyone, sat down, and accepted a cup of coffee from Alice. "Hey, Steve. Thanks, Alice. So, have there been any developments at all with young James?"

Mr. Dean ambled into the room with damp hair and took a seat on the sofa next to his wife. "You must be Jed." He reached across to the armchair and shook hands with the officer. "Steve told me about you. I'm James' father, and I'm afraid we haven't had any luck so far in finding any hint of our boy. There were six of us searching on and off through the night, but I guess he's hiding pretty well."

Jed shrugged. "That could be a good thing in this weather. Hopefully, that means he found somewhere inside to sleep, rather than trying to brave the elements on a park bench or something. This is his first time running away, is that right, Mister Dean?"

"Yes."

Jed nodded slowly. "Many kids come back after the first night or two. They get hungry or bored, or the freedom doesn't seem quite as cool as they envisioned. Steve gave me that photo of James, and I printed it up and handed it around to the guys on duty downtown today."

"Thanks, man." Steve sat cross-legged on the floor. "We appreciate it. A bunch of us will be back out there soon, and hopefully James will surface looking for some breakfast."

"He eats like a horse." Mr. Dean shook his head. "Let's hope his appetite leads him home."

Jed turned to Sara. "Actually, I have some news for you. I know you're probably too overwhelmed to be bothered about your cyber-stalker, but we received confirmation that the recent messages were indeed sent from your high school or the immediate surrounding area. We are looking into yesterday's flowers—Steve texted me about that, and dropped the accompanying card at the station earlier. Someone got creative with that one, and we'll track the information down as quickly as we can."

"You had flowers with a message from that stalker?" Sara's mother gasped. "On top of everything else? Oh Sara, you didn't say anything."

"James is way more important than my messages. Besides, it's nothing life threatening. It's more creepy and unsettling. But it's interesting that the messages might have come from someone at school. I suspected as much, but who on earth would do a thing like that?"

"Has anyone been mean to you at school, sweetheart?" Her father's face was even paler than before.

"No, Dad. In fact, since my singing thing took off, everyone has been super-nice. I was invisible before. Kind of wish I still was, actually."

Jed drained the last of his coffee and stood to leave. "Please keep us informed about James, and give me a shout if you have any more messages, Sara. I'll be praying for you all."

Steve led Jed to the front door and waved him off.

Mr. Dean shook his head. "Another churchy guy, hey? Seems we are surrounded."

Mrs. Dean shrugged. "May not be a bad thing right now, dear."

Sara smiled. When was the last time her mother had

spoken to her dad using a term of endearment? It was a horrific circumstance, and she wished more than anything in the world that James would come home, but the whole ordeal certainly softened her mother's heart.

Steve returned to the room, and passed around a plate laden with toast and peanut butter.

The doorbell made Sara jump from her daydreaming. "I'll get it. You should try to eat, Mom."

She opened the door and was relieved to see Bethany and Todd on the pathway. "Hey, guys. Come on in."

Todd's eyes bugged. "Please tell me that police officer we just passed had some good news?"

"Oh, that was Steve's buddy. He stopped by to check in. No news on James still, I'm afraid."

They both hugged Sara and stood in the doorway of the living room.

"Hey, everyone." Bethany waved shyly. "Hi Mister and Mrs. Dean. This is Todd. He's here to help with the search."

Mr. Dean ushered them inside. "You youngsters are up early. But we're mighty grateful for any help we can get. Have you both eaten?"

"Yes, thank you, sir." Todd shifted from one foot to the other. "When I heard about James, I had to come and look for him. You see, I spent a good chunk of time living on the streets myself when I was about his age. I know a lot of the places kids stay when it's cold."

"You were homeless?" Mrs. Dean's mouth dropped open. "I would never have guessed. Can I ask what brought you back home again?"

"Actually, Pastor Steve did. It's kind of a long story, but he showed me some love, told me about Jesus, and I found hope. My family scene wasn't good, but I turned my life around, and I've been with an awesome foster family for the past several years."

Sara sighed. "I simply don't get why James ran away. It's not like your situation, Todd. He's going through some pre-teen moodiness but he loves his family. I know he does."

Steve refilled the plate with more toast. "We can ask him when he comes home. We have to believe he will come home." He picked up his keys from the coffee table. "Come on, you two. I'll take you downtown and we'll take the first shift looking around. Alice, if you want to come out later with Mister Dean, text me. But for now, honey, I think you should stay and maybe help make some calls."

"Okay." Alice took a slice of toast. "I was thinking of getting some fliers printed, too. I can grab a cab back home and do the printing, change clothes, and pick up my car. That way we'll have an extra vehicle. Is that okay with you, Mister Dean?"

Sara glanced at her father. He wrinkled his nose and shook his head. "I'd rather do something other than sit here. I'm not the most patient man. Can I come with you now, Steve?" He stood and grabbed some toast. "That acceptable with you, ladies?"

Sara nodded. "I'll stay here with Mom and we'll check with James' friends. Someone should be here in case he shows up."

"It's your call, Mister Dean." Steve zipped up his jacket and slid on a pair of leather gloves. "I understand you want to do something, but I don't want you to get sick. You coughed a lot in that cold air early this morning."

"My son's out there, Steve. We have to find him."

Sara walked Bethany out. "Natasha texted and said your flight was pretty rough."

"Yeah." Bethany grimaced. "You can imagine how much Nat enjoyed that. She's sleeping in a bit this morning, but asked if you would call her at nine. We both arranged to take the day off school anyway after the night flight, so she's free to help."

"Thanks." Sara looked up at Todd. "I'd forgotten

about your stint on the streets. You have such an amazing story. I hope you can tell it to James one day." Tears blurred her vision, and she bit her cheek.

"I will. I promise. Go look after your mom and pray, okay?" Todd smiled and followed Steve to the road.

"You have a good guy there," Sara whispered to Bethany.

Instantly, Bethany's face flushed pink. "I know. I'm blessed." She gave Sara a quick hug and trotted down the frozen pathway.

Sara waved at the loaded minivan.

Please, Lord. I don't think my family could handle any more tragedy. I know you are in control, and I know I should be praying something like "your will be done', but James has to be okay. Please.

She rubbed her hands together and hurried back into the warmth.

"Sara?"

"Yes, Mom?"

"Will you pray for James? You know I'm not a religious person, but you all seem to know what you're talking about."

Sara smiled over at Alice, and sat next to her mom, their hands entwined. She prayed out loud for James' safety and for everyone helping with the search. Then she prayed for her parents and her little brothers, who were still fast asleep, blissfully oblivious to the heartache. Finally, she committed the whole situation to her Heavenly Father, knowing He was the miracle worker, and she thanked Him for loving James more than they could possibly imagine.

~ * ~

The day dragged on horribly, and Sara alternated from being her mother's caregiver to being a needy daughter. She paced the carpet so much she almost drove herself crazy. So far none of the team found any clues as to where he might be. Where could he be and why on earth was he doing this to his family?

Mrs. Dean was in the shower at last, so Sara felt free to voice her concerns to Natasha, who arrived with enough pizza to feed an army. "Natasha, what if James isn't even in San Francisco anymore? What if he took off to some other city?"

"Where would he go?" Natasha placed the boxes on the kitchen counter and checked her phone. "The others will be here any minute. It's chilly today—they must be freezing."

Sara stacked some plates next to the pizza. "Maybe he stashed enough money away for a bus ticket or something."

"I thought Steve and Todd already checked the bus station. Didn't they flash around that photo of James? I'm sure someone working there would remember him. We have to believe he's still here somewhere."

Sara sighed. "I don't know anymore."

"Hey, have you put a message out on social media about James yet today?" Natasha had a glint in her eye.

"No. I've been avoiding social media actually, for obvious reasons. Why? Do you think it would help?"

"It's worth a shot, isn't it?" Natasha grabbed Sara's phone from the kitchen table. "Why not put a heartfelt pleading message for your brother to come home? You can ask if anyone has seen him since Saturday, even post his photo. Someone might see it and give you some information to go on. You may get some red herrings, but we're getting desperate here. James might even see it somehow, and then he'll know how worried you are. What do you say?"

Sara shrugged. "I'm willing to do anything to get him home. I don't know why I didn't think of this before. Even if *The Eagle* sees it, I guess there's nothing he can do."

"I know. I'm brilliant." Natasha tossed her long hair over one shoulder and grinned.

Sara heard a key in the lock, and the team quietly took off coats and hats, and filed into the tiny kitchen.

"Sorry, sweetheart." Mr. Dean kissed the top of Sara's head. "No news to report. Where's your mom?"

"She should be finished in the shower any minute. And the boys are spending the night next door with the neighbors. They offered to help out and we thought it would be a good idea. The boys were pretty excited to have a sleepover." She looked up from her phone. "Also, I've posted a message online to see if anyone spotted James in the last couple of days. Maybe it'll jog someone's memory."

"Do you think James might see it?" Mrs. Dean pushed her way into the crowded room, her hair damp and tied in a knot on top of her head.

"I don't know. He didn't have a phone but perhaps he'll go to a library or something to check stuff online. Or he could still be in contact with a friend we don't even know about." Sara opened up the cardboard boxes and the waft of hot cheesy goodness made her stomach growl.

"I know this sounds obvious but has anyone checked James' accounts to see if anything's been posted?" Steve asked, while handing out plates.

"Yeah." Alice opened her laptop. "I've been keeping my eye on it all day. But that doesn't mean he hasn't been on there. He's probably keeping a low profile."

"True." Steve turned to Natasha. "Please thank your parents for all this food. It was very generous of them."

Natasha shrugged. "They wanted to help in some way, but they're both working today, so food seemed like a good idea. Daddy said to let him know if there's anything else they can do."

Sara glanced at her mother. She hunched over the counter with her hand over a trembling mouth. She normally balked at anything to do with the Smithson-Blair family, even after the kindness they showered on Sara. She understood how her family felt second rate in comparison. They lived in two very different worlds. But since Natasha's parents both started their own journey of faith, they were nothing but humble and sweet. Surely her parents could see that now.

Mr. Dean called out from the living room. "Please tell them we are very grateful."

Natasha nodded. "So what's the plan of action? After you've all eaten I mean."

Mr. Dean shouted out again. "Come and sit in here, you guys. Bring your pizza in. I don't know about the rest of you but I need to put my aching feet up for a bit."

"I'll make coffee." Mrs. Dean flicked a switch.

While the team moved into the other room, Sara took down some mugs. Her phone shrilled and she picked it up quickly, hoping to see a response to her plea. There were several messages.

"Anything?" Her mom's eyes begged for good news.

"Let's see. A couple of messages from my friends at school, they say they are really sorry about James. One from my manager, Megan, that says she's still praying. And here's one I don't recognize." Sara's heart dropped.

"What is it?"

Sara lifted a shaky hand and passed the phone to her mom. "*The Eagle* again. Says he hopes my brother never comes home." She shuddered. "Such a creep. Who would say something like that?" She held back a sob.

"Oh, Sara. Why on earth is this person doing this to you?" Mrs. Dean gasped. "You don't suppose he has any- thing to do with James disappearing, do you? How would he even know about James?"

"What's going on in there?" Natasha poked her head around the corner. "Did I hear you mention the dreaded *Ea- gle*?"

Sara joined the others and slumped on the carpet. "Yes, unfortunately. Here, I'll pass my phone around. He says he hopes James never comes home, which obviously means he's still keeping an eye on my social media. I only just put that message up."

Todd bristled. "You don't think your stalker could have any connection with James running away, do you?"

"No. I really don't think so. We've established the fact that James ran away, mainly because he left a note and packed a backpack of stuff. He certainly wasn't taken. Plus, *The Eagle* doesn't say he has him, or knows where he is or anything." Sara wiped at a tear. Exhaustion was kicking in. "Steve, could you let Jed know about this?"

"Of course. I'll call him right away."

Mrs. Dean came behind Sara and gently squeezed her shoulder. Sara managed a weak smile. "It's going to be okay, Mom."

~ * ~

An hour later everyone was warm, full of pizza, and alert after downing numerous cups of coffee. They decided Bethany should spend the night at Natasha's house, as they had to go to school the next day, and both looked exhausted after their weekend in Canada.

Mr. Smithson-Blair picked up the girls, and took a bundle of Alice's fliers to drop at the bus station en route. Steve, Alice, and Todd planned to spend another hour distributing fliers locally before turning in for the night.

"Can I come with you guys this time?" Sara stared at James' photo on the flier. "I could do with some fresh air to clear my head, and we won't be long dropping these around the neighborhood."

Alice looked at Steve. "Sure, we'll be even quicker with four of us, right honey? Todd needs to get home pretty soon, whether he likes it or not." She nudged Todd. "School tomorrow, buddy."

He grimaced.

"You all should go home." Mr. Dean could barely keep his eyes open. "We appreciate all you've done but can't possibly ask any more from you."

Sara's phone rang loudly, causing her to drop the bundle of fliers from her gloved hand.

"Ugh, I'm so klutzy."

She rapidly tugged off one glove and jabbed her phone. "Hello?"

Silence filled the line. She pulled it away from her ear and checked the number, but it wasn't any of her regular contacts.

"Hello? Who's there?"

Everyone gathered around, and Sara's mouth went dry. *The Eagle*—could he be taking his harassment to the next level?

"Sara?" The familiar voice caused her to take a sharp breath.

"James? James, is that really you?"

Sara vaguely heard her mother make a strange sound before she fell into her husband's arms.

"James, where are you? Are you okay?"

Traffic whizzed by in the background, and was followed by a muffled sound, as if the phone was being shifted.

"I phoned to say I'm sorry, Sara. And I'm fine. I'm staying with a friend. I'm not ready to come home yet."

Sara blew a curl from her face. "Okay. Which friend?"

"That doesn't matter. I'm safe. Tell Mom I'm not doing drugs or anything stupid. I needed some space. I really am sorry, Sara."

"You have nothing to be sorry about, James. We all want you to come home. We've been looking for you. Can we pick you up?"

"No. I can't face you yet, Sara. Good-bye."

The line went dead.

Mrs. Dean touched her daughter's arm. "Please say he's coming home?"

Sara stared at her phone, confused but relieved. Everyone asked questions at once, and she fielded them as quickly as she could, but her mind was in a muddle.

"I'm sorry, Mom, but he says he's not ready to come home. He says there's something he's really sorry about."

Mrs. Dean shook her head as tears of relief streamed down her face. "He's probably sorry for putting us through the worry and stress."

Sara chewed her thumbnail. "I'm not so sure. It sounded like he was sorry about something he'd done to me in particular. He said he couldn't face me yet. He's been a bit off recently, but nothing to be all cut up about."

Alice pulled Sara into a hug. "The important thing is he made contact, and you know he's well."

"And that he wants to come home eventually." Todd whistled. "That's huge. And it's good to know he's with a friend."

"You're right." Sara exhaled and put an arm around each of her parents. "This is an answer to prayer. And soon we can ask James all about it, and help him work through the problem, whatever it is."

Mr. Dean wiped at his ruddy face with a large, white handkerchief. "I haven't felt this relieved in years. Thanks again everyone for giving up your time and helping us search for our boy. I guess he doesn't want to be found until he's ready. I suggest we all call it a day and try to get some sleep." He turned to his wife. "Although I'm guessing you will stay by the window. Right, darling?"

Mrs. Dean pulled her husband into a hug and buried her head into his cushy middle.

Alice took out her phone. "I'll text the girls and let them know James called. Steve, could you call the police station and fill them in?"

Steve nodded. "Sure, and then we should leave this family in peace. I guess you are staying here, Sara?"

"Yes. I'll fetch the boys from next door and tell

them the good news. I know he's not home yet, but at least we know he hasn't gone far, and he's physically okay. I think I might go to school in the morning—I could learn something more about James' whereabouts. It's worth a try."

Mr. Dean grimaced. "You sure you want to go in, sweetheart? We still have this *Eagle* character to deal with, remember?"

"It's not like I can forget, Dad." Sara smiled at Alice. "Prayer and peace. I want to face my fears and not live in constant anxiety and frustration. Life's too short."

"Good for you." Mrs. Dean planted a kiss on Sara's forehead. "But be careful. You've come a long way. I'm glad you didn't settle for a quiet life."

Sara's heart felt lighter than it had in a very long time.

She was nobody's mouse.

~ *Fifteen* ~

"*S*o let me get this straight." Natasha's voice boomed through the phone. "James spoke with you and is fine but doesn't want to come home yet. Is that right?"

"Yes." Sara cringed. "Sorry to wake you up so early, Natasha, but I kind of hoped you could swing by here on your way to school with my backpack and some jeans."

"You sure you feel up to going to school today? It's been an intense week, and James is still not home."

"I know. But I think I'll go crazy if I sit around here waiting any more. Besides, I might hear something about James from the kids in school. Lots in my grade have younger siblings, and there are bound to be rumors and gossip about where he might be. But I think I should sleep here with my family until everything's back to normal."

"Of course. No problem. But what about *The Eagle*? Aren't you nervous about being in school, knowing he's got a contact there? Or worse, that he actually goes to your school?"

"Yeah, I'm nervous. But you're the one who's always telling me to face my fears and not be so shy and anxious. Do you think it seems insensitive to go to school with James not home yet?" Sara brushed her curls with one hand and held the phone in the other, and then traded.

Natasha snorted. "Since when am I ever worried about sensitivity? No, I don't want you to get freaked out, that's all. And I miss you not being here. I got used to having you around, and I want everything back to normal. Call me, okay? We'll drop your stuff on the way to my early class. Ciao."

Sara smiled into the mirror. She had some good friends—quirky but good. She patted a little foundation under her eyes, in an attempt to disguise the dark rings caused by lack of sleep, and smeared on some lip-gloss. Natasha would be impressed. She took a deep breath and stared at her reflection.

You can do this. It's only school. Oh, Lord—"when I am afraid, I put my trust in you".

~ * ~

By lunchtime, Sara began to relax. A few classmates asked how the concert went, and handsome Adam Tromness flirted with her in math. There were no murmurs about James, but she guessed the kids in her grade weren't that bothered by a runaway in middle school.

She pulled out her sandwich and set it on the cafeteria table while she waited for her usual lunch girls to arrive. They weren't super close, but all of them were straight A students, mostly shy, and the topic of conversation was always interesting. They would ask about her photo shoot out of politeness, and then most likely discuss the merits of Shakespeare or something.

Sara gazed through the window to the parking lot, and noticed a police car. Her stomach clenched. There were two officers, one male and one female, along with a middle-aged woman, who was visibly distraught.

"What's going on out there?" Some boy from the next table peered over Sara's shoulder.

"I don't know." Suddenly, her peanut butter and jelly sandwich didn't seem very appealing. She craned her neck to see if she recognized the woman.

The school buzzer sounded, and a nasally voice made an announcement:

"Could Sara Dean please report to the principal's office?"

Sara's head spun. Was there news of James? She stood, stuffed her lunch in her backpack, and hurried from the cafeteria, knowing all eyes were watching her. She kept her head down, and tried not to bump into anyone while she rushed down the corridor. Was James safe? Who on earth was that woman with the police?

In less than two minutes, she reached Principal Murray's office, and knocked twice on the open door.

"Come in."

Sara had never been in this room before. It was surprisingly spacious, and not the usual bland décor one would expect. Modern art hung on the walls and the chairs were bright red. Principal Murray was a no-nonsense sort of man. He always gave the impression of being a mix between angry and in pain—his bushy eyebrows met in the middle, and his thin lips puckered like he was sucking a lemon.

"Please, come in and take a seat, Sara. Close the door behind you."

Sara clumsily dropped her backpack to the floor with a thud and lowered herself into one of the funky red chairs. In the seat next to her, the woman from the police car scrunched a wad of Kleenex™, and on her other side was Brittany Wade, a girl in Sara's class. The two police officers stood at attention on the far side of the room.

Sara took a deep breath, and waited for her principal to explain what was going on. He folded his arms, sat back in his chair, and squinted first at Brittany and then at Sara.

"Do you know why you are here, Sara?"

She felt her face heat up instantly, and her stomach flipped. "No, sir. I thought maybe there was news about my little brother. He ran away this weekend."

Principal Murray puckered his mouth. "I'm afraid this is regarding another matter." He leaned over his desk and made a steeple shape with his hands. "Do you know Brittany Wade very well?"

Sara turned and looked at the girl. She knew Brittany vaguely from choir in their younger grades but had she ever had a conversation with her? Brittany's eyes were fixed on her own hands in her lap, which were visibly shaking. Her

120

short, black hair was styled in a shiny bob, and Sara noticed a subtle nose piercing. Her tall, slim frame was dressed immaculately as usual—Sara often appreciated her unique sense of style.

"Um, not really. We used to sing in choir together, and we've been in most of the same school productions. I don't think we have any of the same classes this year though. Is there a problem?"

Brittany was as still as a statue, other than her shaking hands.

Principal Murray nodded toward the police officers. "It seems the authorities have reason to believe Miss Wade is harassing you."

Confusion clouded Sara's mind, and for a moment all words lodged in her throat.

The female police officer stepped closer to the desk and placed a clipboard of papers in front to Sara. "I'm Officer Donaldson, Sara. This is a printout of the messages you received recently, and the flower card. We managed to get details of the sender from your flower delivery last Sunday. There was rather flimsy paper trail, and it all led back to a credit card belonging to Wendy Wade, Brittany's mother."

Mrs. Wade shook her head and blew her nose. "I had no idea." She turned to look straight at Sara. "I'm so sorry about all of this. It came as a complete shock."

"I'm really confused." Sara looked from Mrs. Wade to Officer Donaldson. "Brittany never harassed me. I've been cyber-stalked by some creepy *Eagle* guy, but there must be some mistake."

Brittany snapped her head up and glared at Sara. "There's no mistake, you silly little mouse. You still don't get it, do you?"

Mouse?

Sara gasped and gripped both armrests to steady herself. *The Eagle* wasn't a guy?

Mrs. Wade put a firm hand on her daughter's arm. "You might want to tread carefully here. You're already in a lot of trouble, please don't make it any worse."

"You're *The Eagle*?" Sara's mouth dropped open. "But... why? What have I ever done to you, Brittany? I barely even know you."

"You really have no idea? How can you be so naïve? Ever since seventh grade, you got the best singing parts in choir and all our major performances. I used to be number one before you decided to try out for choir, and suddenly, I was old news. It didn't matter that I devoted all my free time to vocal coaches and singing lessons. You appeared one day with zero experience and one hundred percent natural talent, and ever since then I've tried everything to be better than you."

Sara's eyes opened wide. "You are jealous of me? That's why?"

The harsh edge disappeared from Brittany's voice. "Yes, the green-eyed monster chasing the turquoise-eyed successful singer. So now you know." She slumped down lower in her chair.

The adults in the room were silent.

Sara couldn't breathe. It didn't make sense. Her cheeks flushed with anger at the pain Brittany caused by her jealousy but at the same time her heart melted at the tone of desperation in Brittany's voice. Sara leaned across Mrs. Wade and put a hand on Brittany's arm.

"I'm sorry."

"You're sorry?" Brittany sneered. "Why, are you going to end my future right now by sending me to jail or something?"

"No, of course not. I'm sorry I caused you to feel so low, and I'm sorry you didn't think I was approachable. I would have willingly shared any of those lead roles with you. I know you have a fantastic voice, and believe it or not, I hate being in the limelight."

Principal Murray cleared his throat. "That's awfully gracious of you, Sara. I must say you have a very forgiving attitude. I know this whole ugly situation caused untold grief. It's our hope that we can resolve most of this here. I'm happy to meet with your parents. We could call them now if you would like."

"No, Principal Murray, please don't phone my parents. Today they are dealing with my brother's disappearance. Quite honestly, I'm relieved I know who my stalker is now. At least I won't have to second guess every guy who walks past me anymore." She turned back to Brittany. "I have to ask—why call yourself *The Eagle*?"

Brittany shrugged. "I got the idea from your music binder. You have that massive Bible verse printed on the front. I even memorized it: *'but those who hope in the Lord will renew their strength. They will soar on wings like eagles; they will run and not grow weary, they will walk and not be faint.'* I figured you saw yourself as some eagle flying high above the rest of us, so I wanted to put you in your place."

Sara gasped. "Oh, no. It's not meant to be a bragging verse, Brittany. It's pointing to God being our hope and giving us strength."

"Whatever."

"Okay, so that's *The Eagle* name, but how did you know my whereabouts and stuff? Were you actually following me? You went to a huge amount of trouble merely to freak me out."

Mrs. Wade sighed. "Brittany's father up and left us last year. I know it's absolutely no excuse for her behavior but it's been devastating for both of us. She's been a little irrational."

"Mom, I can't blame Dad for this. Or you. I've been jealous of Sara for years, and you poured a fortune into my singing. My dream has always been to sing professionally." She turned angry eyes on Sara. "When you fell into an amazing contract with those Gracelight people, and were so humble and shy about the whole thing, I guess I blew my lid."

"Are you sorry?" Principal Murray glared straight at Brittany.

She waited for several seconds, glanced at Sara, and nodded. "Yes, I am now. It got out of hand. I was only going to message you once, to freak you out a bit. It was an easy way to get to you." She jutted her chin. "I accept whatever punishment you give me. You can't take away my voice, and that's what keeps my dream alive, so do what you want. But there's something you should know, Sara."

Sara held her breath, afraid of any more surprises. "Yes?"

"I didn't do this alone. I had an accomplice, if you can call him that."

Sara's head spun. Who on earth would want to hurt her like this? Another random student she hardly knew? Adam Tromness even? Her pulse quickened until she couldn't bear to wait another second.

"Who is it?"

Brittany sneered. "Your elusive little brother, James."

~ Sixteen ~

Sara felt nauseous and her head was ready to explode. After *The Eagle* revelation, she wanted to go home and explain everything to her parents, before word spread about James' involvement. The police officers offered her a ride, and now she felt like a criminal as curious passersby craned to see who occupied the back seat of the police car. It was the height of irony.

"My home is around the next bend, Officer."

The driver slowed down outside her house.

Officer Donaldson rushed out and opened the door for Sara. "Would you like us to explain everything to your parents?"

Sara grabbed her backpack and turned to the driver. "Thanks. But would you mind if only one of you came in with me? They might get a bit overwhelmed. It's been a tough week."

"I'll wait out here." The driver pulled out his notebook. "You two go ahead and let me know if you need me."

Before they reached the front door, Mr. Dean opened it wide, his face gray. "What's wrong? Is it James?"

"No, Dad, nothing awful happened. We need to talk though. Is Mom here?"

"Yes, she's in the kitchen. Come on in."

They all settled in the living room, and Officer Donaldson told them about Brittany. They discussed what appropriate steps should be taken regarding punishment, and decided to sleep on it. Finally, Sara plucked up the courage to tell them about James.

"I think I know why James ran away." She clutched her mom's hand. "Brittany said James helped her."

"Helped her how?" Mrs. Dean looked like she had been slapped.

"He let her know when I was going anywhere special, he told her the details of my Canada trip, and fed her whatever information she wanted."

Mr. Dean stood and half-paced, half-hobbled around the small room. "Why? What would make him do a thing like that? He must know how upset you were about the whole ordeal. No wonder he's scared to come home. How did he even know a girl from high school? Was she paying him or something?"

Sara nodded. "A little. Brittany told me James was ticked at me and didn't have a problem helping her out."

"Oh, Sara." Mrs. Dean burst into tears. "I can't imagine how this must feel for you—your own brother. I can't believe it. He loves you so much. Whatever has gotten into that boy?"

"It's okay, Mom. I think he's mad at me for leaving home. I'll talk with him and we'll smooth it out. I need to try to make contact with him as soon as possible. Let him know I've discovered the truth, and that he can come home. I've already forgiven him."

Mrs. Dean shook her head. "He doesn't deserve your forgiveness. Maybe not yet, at least."

"None of us really deserve forgiveness, Mom." Sara smiled. "But that's the great thing about being a Christian. You get to understand a little bit about grace and mercy through God. I'm simply trying to show love toward James in the same way God loves me, even when I mess up."

Officer Donaldson cleared her throat and stood. "I think I'll leave you all to your discussion now. Please let us know once James comes home. I'm optimistic you can resolve this. You're a strong young lady, Sara." She turned to Mr. and Mrs. Dean. "Don't hesitate to call, and perhaps we can talk again tomorrow and discuss the best course of action to take with Brittany."

"Thank you." Sara walked her to the front door and waved to the other officer in the car. When she returned to the living room, her parents were motionless, and both stared into space.

"You guys look so tired. Why don't you try and take a nap? I'll stay here and listen for the phone. I'll be around for Jake and Timothy when they get home from school, too. Go on, I promise I'll come and wake you if there's any news."

Mrs. Dean smoothed her hair from her forehead. "Maybe for an hour. I think we all need to let this information sink in." She stood and stretched. "Thank you."

"You too, Dad." Sara pulled him up and he limped to the hallway.

"You sure you don't want some company, sweetheart?" He scrunched up his face and glanced from the hallway to his daughter.

"No. Actually a little alone time would be nice. I'm going to put a message out there for James, too. He has to know I'm not mad with him now that I know the truth, and that he's welcome home."

"I'm proud of you." Mr. Dean blew her a kiss and ambled away in the direction of the bedrooms.

Sara sank into the ancient armchair. She rubbed her hands across the worn arms and decided to buy her parents a new recliner for Christmas. Hopefully, they wouldn't see it as an insult, but as a gift from the heart. This music career was going to be a difficult road to travel if it escalated as Megan predicted, but there had to be some understanding on both sides. She shrugged. Material possessions were never a priority, although the thought of being able to bless others with special presents occasionally made her heart flutter. Maybe she would be able to afford to send her brothers to summer camp or something.

James.

Her head ached wondering where on earth he was. It hurt to think he would accept money from Brittany. Why would he want to upset his own sister? Surely he knew better than most how fearful and anxious she was. She always had been. Many times he was the one to persuade her to step up and take a role in a school production or do something that took courage, even though he was the younger sibling. She rubbed her tired eyes. They felt like they were covered in grit.

"Tea. I need peppermint tea."

Sara wandered over to the kitchen and flicked on the kettle. She pulled out her phone and quickly texted Natasha, Bethany, and Alice, filling them in on the basics. Natasha replied right away, and suggested they meet up that evening at Alice's place, as it was fairly central. From there they could head downtown for another quick search for James, if he hadn't turned up by then. The plan was confirmed.

While the tea steeped and gave off a deliciously soothing scent, Sara realized she was hungry. She dug out the sandwich she hadn't eaten at lunch from her backpack, and took a bite. Peanut butter and jelly was James' favorite. She quickly made two more and wrapped them up. She would take them out tonight when they searched for him. He would be hungry for sure. And cold. She shivered, even though the kitchen was toasty warm.

Sara sent up a quick prayer for wisdom, and then wrote a private message to James on his Facebook account, hoping he would have the opportunity to read it somehow:

> "Hey James—I know about
> Brittany being my stalker,
> and she told me you helped her.
> But it's okay. I forgive you. Truly.
> PLEASE come home. We need to
> talk. I miss you. xoxo"

She sipped her tea and leaned against the counter. Through the grubby kitchen window, she watched a tiny brown bird peck the solid ground. He was desperate for food, and determined to keep pecking. Just like she would keep looking for James, for as long as it would take.

Her phone suddenly blared with her favorite song, and she quickly picked up, so as not to disturb her parents.

"Hello?"

There was no answer, but someone was definitely on the other end.

At first, Sara froze at the thought of *The Eagle*, but the next second she remembered Brittany's confession, and the fact that there was no stalker out there. The call could be from her brother.

"James? Is that you?"

"Hey."

His voice sounded so young, so vulnerable.

"James, it's really you. Did you see my message? Listen to me. I meant what I said, I'm not mad at you or anything. We all want you to come home. Mom and Dad and your brothers all miss you like crazy. So do I. Can we come and pick you up?"

Silence.

"James?"

"I can't face you, Sara. I feel like such a loser. Plus, now everyone knows what I've done. It'll be all around school."

"You're not in trouble. I don't understand why you did it but I love you regardless."

Sara heard quiet sniffling.

"James, are you still staying with a friend? At least let me know you are safe."

"I'm fine. But I have to leave here soon. His mom didn't even know I was crashing in her basement 'cause she works double shifts but she's getting suspicious now, so once I've hung up, I'm out of here."

"Come home?"

"Not yet. It doesn't feel right. Nobody understands."

A thought hit Sara from out of the blue. "Wait, will you meet up with Todd? You know, from my youth group? You've met him before. He's really cool and he actually spent a long time living on the streets when he was your age."

"Seriously?"

"Yeah. Can he meet you tonight? Say at six?"

"I guess. But only Todd, okay? Not Mom or Dad. Tell him I'll meet him outside the main library. I can walk there. But if I see anyone else with him, I'll run. Sorry, sis."

"I understand. Please be there. I think Todd can help. He's a great listener, too."

"Bye."

"Bye, James."

Sara exhaled, and then hurried to report the news to her parents. Then she would call Todd and pray he was free tonight.

~ Seventeen ~

"*O*h my goodness, your poor parents must be going crazy at home." Alice ushered Sara through her front door and into the foyer. She took the dripping wet coat and hung it up to dry. "Too bad it decided to pour with rain this evening."

Sara shrugged. "Hopefully James found somewhere warm and dry to hang out for a few hours. I hate to think of him outside in this weather. Is Todd here yet?"

"Yes, of course." Alice followed her inside. Everyone was anxiously waiting—Steve, Todd, Bethany, and Natasha all sat in the living room awaiting instructions.

"Come on in." Natasha beckoned Sara to squash in between her and Bethany on the sofa. "We want to know what's going on, and what you want us all to do." Her hands flew up in the air. "This is so wild."

"I know." Sara pulled the tie from her hair, allowing her curls to escape and dry off a little. "Todd, I hate to put all this pressure on you, but you were the first name that popped into my mind when James said he wouldn't speak to me face-to-face yet."

"No problem." Todd pushed up the sleeves of his sweatshirt. "I'm sure it's a God thing. Fill me in. You know I want to see James back home where he belongs. But I also understand he feels skittish, and maybe I can hang out with him for a while and see what's eating him up."

"Exactly." Sara pursed her lips. "Unfortunately, James said he'd only show up if Todd is alone. If I go, I think he'll run again."

Alice scooted closer to Steve on the loveseat. "This must be tough on your parents, Sara—knowing their son will meet with Todd, but doesn't want to see them yet. I'm surprised they are letting us do this, to be honest."

"They really don't have much choice, honey." Steve spoke calmly. "James is calling the shots, and if they want him home safe and sound, they need to be patient. I'm pretty sure they trust us now."

Sara glanced down at her chewed up fingernails. "They're both a mess. Of course they're relieved James is willing to meet someone, it's a step in the right direction at least. But it's frustrating. They desperately want him home. I promised to keep them up to date with every-thing."

Natasha leaned forward. "So Todd is going on his own?"

"I'll give him a ride." Steve jangled his keys. "He's got to get downtown somehow. But I'll stay in my van un-less Todd signals me to do otherwise. The parking lot should be quiet at six. The library stays open until eight. Right, Alice?"

"Yes, you'll have plenty of time. Todd, I think you should hang out on one of the benches outside. Some of them are below that huge overhang, so you should be shel-tered from the rain. That way Steve can keep an eye on you, but give James his space. Go inside the library if it's too cold and he wants to talk." Alice turned to Sara. "Do you think your parents will be cool with that? I want them to be involved in all this."

"That sounds like a good plan to me. I'm texting my dad right now to explain." Sara looked up from her phone. "Should the rest of us wait here?" She sighed. "I wish I could go, too. I want to give him a big hug and tell him I'm not mad."

Todd stood and picked up his backpack. "I'll tell him what happened, and that you're not angry with him. But if I do manage to talk him into coming home right away, I think you should be back at your parents' place."

Bethany passed Todd his baseball cap. "Maybe we

should make our way over to the Deans' home. We could wait there with them, for moral support."

"You're right." Sara handed the package of peanut butter and jelly sandwiches to Todd. "But once the guys leave, let's stay here for a little while and pray for this crazy meeting. Pray for my parents, too. Do you mind?"

"Great idea." Alice kissed Steve's cheek and then ushered both guys out into the cold, wet evening. The girls huddled around the crackling fire and offered heartfelt prayers to their Heavenly Father, as if their lives depended on it—because James' life could well be in the balance.

~ * ~

Later, back at her family home, Sara checked her phone yet again. It was six-thirty, and they hadn't heard anything since Steve's call at six o'clock. The rain was heavy, so Todd and James were both inside the library, after an awkward high-five and an initial conversation on the bench. That was thirty minutes ago.

Natasha's foot tapped against the coffee table, and Mr. Dean paced the living room like a madman. Alice was on tea duty with Bethany, and Mrs. Dean curled up on the sofa, flanked by her two youngest boys, who were uncharacteristically quiet.

Sara patted little Timothy's knee. "Would you boys like some cookies? Bethany baked chocolate chip and brought some over for us."

"Really?" Timothy's blue eyes brightened, and he scurried into the kitchen.

"Bring one for me, too." Jake grinned.

"You okay, Mom?" Sara sat in Timothy's place on the sofa.

"I will be. Once James is home. What do you suppose they're talking about? I can barely get more than one-syllable answers from him most of the time."

Sara smiled. "Todd's great at getting people to open up. Right, Bethany?"

Bethany walked in with a tray of steaming mugs, followed by Timothy, who carried a large plate of cookies.

"Yeah, I have to admit, he's got that gift of being able to talk to anyone and make them feel comfortable. It's the very first thing I noticed about him."

Natasha snorted. "Like the intense hunky good looks didn't grab you first."

Bethany blushed. "Natasha."

Suddenly, Sara's phone burst into song and she almost dropped it. "Hello? Steve, what's happening?"

"Someone wants to speak to you, Sara. Here, let me pass the phone over to him."

Sara switched to speakerphone so everyone in the room could hear.

"James, are you there?"

"Hey, Sara. I'm here. I talked with Todd."

"And?"

"He's a pretty cool guy."

"I told you so." Sara looked at the faces around her, each one wide-eyed and holding their breath. "Are you coming home?"

James gulped and Sara's heart melted.

"Are you sure you want me there, Sara? Todd says you forgave me and aren't mad. I don't blame you if you never want to see me again. I'm such a jerk. But I miss everyone."

Mrs. Dean sobbed and put her hands over her mouth.

"Please come home." Sara sniffed. "I love you."

A draft blew in from the entrance porch, and Sara stood and twisted to see if the front door had blown open from the storm. The door was wide open, and James stood perfectly still, the phone at his ear.

"I love you, too, sis."

"Oh, James." Sara threw her phone onto the sofa and in three strides she smothered her brother with a bear hug. Pandemonium broke out in the Deans' living room, and cheers erupted when Sara dragged James into the center of the room amidst hugs and tears.

Mrs. Dean held him at arms' length and studied him. "You look tired, son. Have you eaten? Jake, please go and run a bath for your brother." She peeled off his coat, hat and scarf, and pulled him onto the sofa next to her. "You know you just about worried us to death, don't you?"

Mr. Dean couldn't even speak. He buried his head in his eldest boy's hair and held on tightly.

James looked smaller than Sara remembered. He was pale, and dark shadows lay beneath his eyes, but other than that, he appeared to be fine. She thanked God for His protection.

"Hey, everyone." James turned sheepishly to each person gathered. "I want to apologize to you all. I'm sorry for making you worry and stuff. Todd told me how you've been searching for me and praying and all that." He sighed heavily. "I know I was a jerk to run away, but I panicked." His eyes found Sara's. "And I felt guilty for helping that Brittany girl scare you." He bowed his head. "I don't even know why I did it. I feel horrible."

Sara rustled his blonde mop of hair. "I'm glad you're back where you belong. What made you decide to come home?"

"Todd told me about the time he ran away. It was way different, and I realized I have it pretty good at home here. Then he told me this story about a boy in the Bible who ran away and messed up, and his dad still welcomed him home after he'd really hurt him, because he loved him.

"He also said that's how God is with us, even when we mess up. You told me that before. But the story reminded me of you, Sara. How you said you forgave me and still love me, and that I should come home anyway." He swiftly wiped his eyes in his sleeve. "Thank you."

Sara pulled him into her arms and let him cry. Steve, Alice, Todd, Bethany and Natasha all stood and mouthed their goodbyes. Her parents walked them to the door and she heard them express their sincere thanks. While James sobbed, Sara's heart soared. God even worked this fearful situation into something good. His love was so evident through her friends, and surely this would speak volumes to her family.

"When I am afraid, I put my trust in You." She whispered the words into her brother's curly hair and breathed a sigh of relief. Jake and Timothy scampered around the house, sugared up from the cookies. Her mom cried tears of joy in the kitchen and made more tea, and her dad was on the phone, probably spreading the good news.

"Sara?" James pulled away and looked intently into her eyes. "Making you afraid was the meanest thing I could ever do. I guess I was jealous of all the nice stuff you had at Natasha's place, or maybe it was because you were like, famous. I was kind of mad that you left home. I miss you." He puffed out his chest. "But I can take any punishment you and Mom and Dad think I should get. I'm man enough." His face dropped. "I won't have to go to prison, will I?"

"No, of course not, silly. I'll chat with Mom and Dad, but I think you've learned some valuable lessons through all this."

"What about Brittany?"

"We met in the Principal's office today, and I said we would sleep on it and decide if we want to take it any further. How did you even know her anyway?"

James picked at a dirty Band-Aid on his thumb. "Those guys who hang out across the street. She's a cousin to one of them. It's a long story."

"And we have lots of time to get through all this some other time. Right now, why don't you go and take a bath? You don't smell too great. You can even use my bubble bath. Can I make you something to eat?"

James grinned sheepishly. "Any chance I could have another peanut butter and jelly sandwich?"

"Absolutely."

"Thank you, sis." James trudged to the hallway and turned back. "For everything."

~ * ~

After the best night's sleep in a very long time, Sara woke to the obnoxious beep of her alarm. She opened her eyes and slapped the clock. She didn't want it to wake James in the next room. He needed to spend this morning in bed to recover from his tumultuous week.

She had spoken with her parents last night before bed, and they agreed with her decision about Brittany. Sara smiled. She needed to phone the girl and meet up with her as soon as possible.

She tiptoed down to the kitchen, flicked on the kettle, and pulled out the school directory from the junk drawer. It didn't take long to find Brittany's home number, and Sara decided seven-thirty wasn't too early to call. She pulled the phone from her robe pocket, typed in the number, and held her breath.

"Hello?" Sara recognized Brittany's mother's voice.

"Hi, Mrs. Wade, this is Sara Dean from school. I'm sorry to phone so early, but I wanted to catch Brittany."

There was an awkward silence. "Of course, Sara. Yes, Brittany is right here. She didn't sleep much last night, and I know she's anxious to hear from you. I'll pass you over."

"Thanks, Mrs. Wade."

"Hi Sara." Brittany sounded upset. "I didn't know you would phone me in person. I thought those cops would be in touch or Principal Murray."

"I'm going to phone them later this morning and let them know what I've decided. Listen, Brittany, we both know what you did was wrong and cruel, but I meant what I said—I do forgive you."

"Okay. But I guess there is a 'but' here."

"No. It makes me sad to think you're a singer like

me, and we've never even hung out together or had a decent conversation."

"What? Okay, I'm a bit confused here."

Sara took a deep breath. This was her chance to reach out and show love and forgiveness. "I'm dropping any charges or accusations. I'm not taking this any further, not even with our principal."

"Seriously?"

"Yes. I really want to try and find something positive in all this mess. I would like to speak with Miss Davies and start a mentoring model in our school choir. Older, more mature singers like you and I will take the newbies under our wing and invest some time to help and encourage them. I hope it will diffuse any jealousy or feelings of not being good enough amongst the group. When everyone sees us working together as friends, this whole mess will be history, and it'll be the start of a great initiative in choir for the future."

Brittany was quiet for several seconds. "I like that idea. I think I would have benefitted from something like that in the earlier grades. But you want to be my... friend?" She sounded horrified.

"That sounds a bit cheesy, but I honestly think we have a lot in common, and that we can help each other with our singing. Put *The Eagle* behind us. What do you say?"

"I say you are crazy." Brittany laughed a pretty, melodious laugh. "And that you are very kind. My mom's not going to believe this. She's already banned me from social media, and I'm grounded for a ridiculous amount of time, but she promised not to touch my singing. It's precious to me."

"I understand that."

"But Sara, what about James? Have you heard from him or anything? I feel like I should take the blame for that, too."

"James is currently fast asleep in his bed—forgiven, loved, and exhausted. We sorted it out."

"For real? Man, that's the best. I know I used him when he felt vulnerable for whatever reason, but he really is a cute kid. He should stay away from my cousin, by the way. He's bad news. But I'm super glad James is okay."

"Me too. Hey, I should get ready for school, but you know where to find me at lunch if you're not completely weirded out talking to me in public. We should go and speak with Miss Davies at choir and tell her about the mentorship thing."

"Sara, I don't think we are ever going to be besties, but I appreciate what you are doing. And I'm grateful that you're not dragging me through the mud with all this. Rumors in school are going to be unbearable." Her voice cracked.

"Hey, don't you worry about what others say. It'll be yesterday's news in no time. I'm not going to put you down in front of others, Brittany. I believe we all need grace."

"Whatever. I can't imagine you ever need it."

"Oh no, you have that all wrong. I need grace as much as the next person. You can ask my brothers. I'll see you later, okay?"

"Sure. And for the record, Sara, I had the mouse thing all wrong."

"Thanks, Brittany."

"No. Thank you, Sara Dean."

~ *Eighteen* ~

*S*ara's stomach churned with familiar pre-performance butterflies. She only had a few precious minutes of solitude left until well-wishers would invade the green room.

This Christmas concert was something she had looked forward to for weeks, especially after all the recent drama in her life. Megan pulled together a fantastic event, and Natasha's mom was a marketing queen. This was Sara's biggest concert to date—hence the butterflies.

"Knock, knock?" Sara's dad and three brothers descended upon her tranquility. She laughed when the two younger boys swarmed her, wrapping their arms around her middle, each jostling for attention.

"Boys, mind your sister's posh outfit." Mr. Dean winked. He tore the boys away and admired her evening dress. "Stunning. You look like a princess."

Sara's face heated. "Thanks, Dad." She gave him a peck on his bristly cheek. "You scrubbed up rather well yourself."

He shrugged. "I do possess one suit for very special occasions. Although your mother had to let out the button on my waistband a tad."

James leaned in and gave Sara a hug. "I can't wait to hear you sing on stage, sis. This is pretty cool. Some of the guys from school are even coming."

"Really? That's awesome, James. Hey, where is Mom?"

"Oh, don't worry, she said she'll stop by in a minute. She wanted to thank Alice for the wedding invitation." He turned to his father. "Guess you'll be needing that suit again, Dad. Better not eat too much over Christmas."

"What a cheek." Mr. Dean sucked in his gut and grinned. "Steve and Alice are like family to us now, but we were shocked to receive an invite. Your mother is particularly excited to see you as bridesmaid. We haven't been to a wedding in years. Anyway, we should leave you in peace and go find our seats. We're so proud of you, sweetheart. You go break a leg, or whatever it is you're supposed to say these days."

Sara giggled. "Thanks, Dad. Hope you enjoy the concert, guys. I'll see you afterwards, okay?"

They all waved and Sara smiled to herself as the boys squabbled their way down the corridor.

She took some time to practice her vocal exercises and warm up her voice. This was going to be the longest event yet, and she had to pace herself vocally.

"Ah, that's what I like to hear." Sara immediately recognized her manager's voice. Megan always took care of the details and made everything run like clockwork, which allowed Sara to focus on her singing.

"Hi, Megan, I'm so glad you popped in to see me." She gave her a quick hug. "How's it looking out there? Is everything okay? Any problems? Are there many in the audience?"

"Calm down, sweetheart, everything is perfect." Megan tapped something on her iPad. "It's full to capacity, the stage looks amazing, and the band are all warmed up and ready to roll. How are you doing?"

Sara tilted her head from side to side and rotated her shoulders. "Good. The usual nerves and I'm a bit tense, but I feel really excited about tonight."

"Lots of people are praying for you, and for the words of your songs. I hear a crowd from your high school are coming, and I'm sure they're curious about your faith and why you sing this stuff."

Sara's eyes filled with tears. "Don't make me cry,

Megan. Natasha will shoot me if I ruin this make-up." She took a deep breath. "Maybe you could pray that I don't dissolve into a puddle of mush on stage? It's been an emotional month, and I'm even more tearful than usual."

Megan squeezed her hand. "There's nothing wrong with tears. And you can be vulnerable on stage, you know."

"I know, but preferably not the 'sniveling wreck' version. It would be nice if I could at least get through the songs, so the words are loud and clear."

"You will, Sara. You're stronger than you think."

"Hmm. I've heard that a lot recently."

Megan raised her perfectly shaped eyebrows. "It's true."

"Only because of God. He's the strong One."

"But you know where to turn to find your strength."

"Hello, can we come in?" Alice and Steve stood hand-in-hand at the open door.

"Yes, come on in." Megan greeted them at the door. "You guys must be so excited. Only a couple of weeks until the wedding, right?"

Steve pulled Alice close. "Twenty days to go—not that I'm counting."

Alice positively glowed. She reached up and kissed her fiancé on the cheek.

Megan shook her head. "Way too cute." She gave Sara one last hug. "I have to go and check on a few last minute details. I'll be praying all the way through the concert. It's going to be amazing. I'll catch up with you later. Bye, guys."

Alice let go of Steve's hand and rushed over to Sara. "Here, I wanted to give you this tonight."

Sara took the large shiny, gold bag stuffed with ivory tissue paper and set it on a chair.

"Whatever is this?"

"Open it and find out."

Sara peered into the bag and spotted a white, lacquered picture frame. She carefully pulled it out and the tissue fluttered to the floor.

"Oh, my goodness, Alice. This is spectacular. Thank you so much."

She held an enlargement of one of the photographs Alice took at the Canadian ski resort. It was the one Sara particularly loved, where Alice captured the magical combination of falling snowflakes and the light in Sara's turquoise eyes.

"It was my favorite, hands-down." Alice tucked a strand of hair behind her ear. "And Gracelight is using this one for their promotions, too."

"Really?" Sara's mouth trembled and she fought to hold back tears. "I love it. Thank you so much."

"You're a natural in front of the camera, Sara." Steve admired the shot. "Anyone would think you have done this kind of thing for years."

"Oh no, Steve. I was the farthest thing you can imagine from natural. This was all Alice. You're future wife has some serious talent."

"I agree." He shared a smile with Alice. "But speaking of serious talent, are you ready for tonight's show?"

Sara shuddered. "Yeah, I think so. I know you guys will pray. You have no idea how much I appreciate that."

Alice took the picture frame and slid it back in the bag. "Here, I'll leave this in the corner with your other stuff. You look really gorgeous, Sara. We are both so incredibly proud of you. Right, honey?"

Steve nodded, and his eyes glistened. "You bet we are. We've watched you grow into an amazing, godly young woman. You've handled this fame thing in the most levelheaded, humble way ever. God bless you, Sara."

They both embraced her quickly, and then closed the door behind them and hurried off to the auditorium.

Sara barely had chance to take a swig of water when the door flew open again, and Natasha breezed in toting her make-up bag, closely followed by Bethany and the curling iron.

"Last minute touch-ups." Natasha grinned.

"You guys are the best team ever. You've already performed a fabulous transformation with me. This ugly duckling is feeling very swan-like."

Bethany wagged a finger. "There is nothing 'ugly duckling' about you, ever. You look fantastic, but you are always beautiful."

Natasha dumped her make-up kit on a chair and put both hands on her hips. "But I kind of see where you're coming from with the whole swan thing."

She turned Sara around to face the huge mirror. The effect was quite magnificent. She wore a fitted, long winter-white dress to blend with the snowflake theme of the event. It was something Sara would never choose for herself, but Natasha was convinced the shimmering outfit would be perfect, and she was right. Sara looked more stunning than ever before.

"You did it again, girls." She put an arm around each of her friends. "Thank you both." She sighed deeply. "I wish you could dance on stage with me tonight. That was so amazing in Vancouver."

"It was." Bethany checked Sara's dress was straight. "But Gracelight wanted it to be simple and all you this evening. I think it was a good decision. It looks really Christmassy out there. You're doing some carols, right?"

"Yes, a few actually. I'm finishing with '*O Holy Night*'."

Bethany gasped. "That's my favorite. I remember you singing it a cappella at Steve's Christmas bonfire party almost two years ago. It spoke to us both that night. Right, Nat?"

Natasha nodded. "Actually, that was the first time I heard you sing. I knew you would go far. By the way, your new friend Brittany is sitting next to us at the front, just so you know."

"Really? Brittany showed up? That's great." Sara tried not to move while Natasha perfected the eyeliner. "I appreciate your help with her. Now that I know her a little, she's actually a super nice girl."

Natasha huffed. "She wasn't super nice when she was stalking you. But the girl's got pipes, I'll give her that."

"Yeah, her voice is really good. She was so grateful when Megan gave her those contacts. I really think she's got a good shot in the music industry one day."

"But not with Gracelight?" Bethany smoothed a ringlet. "Oh, I guess she doesn't want to sing Christian material."

"Not yet." Sara waggled her eyebrows. "I'm praying about that one. I know Natasha had some good conversations with her, too."

"I sure did. She's blown away with how gracious and forgiving you were toward her, Sara. That 'actions speak louder than words' thing is true. A warning and a ban from her social media was pretty light punishment, and she's actually enjoying the mentorship choir program. She's really grateful."

"What about James?" Bethany stood back to admire her handiwork. "How's he doing?"

Sara smiled broadly. "I've never seen him happier. Even though he's grounded for a fair chunk of time, his relationship with Mom and Dad is so much better, and in school he's hanging out with his old friends again, the good kids. Plus he's a total keener at Youth now. Todd is his mentor, and he wants to know everything about God. I can't believe it. Hey, isn't tomorrow the big day for you?"

Bethany blushed, and then swiped at a tear. "Yeah. It's bittersweet though. My birthday will always be painful. How do you ever get over losing both parents on your birthday?"

"Oh, Bethany. I'm so sorry." Sara hugged her friend. "Of course it's painful. I feel awful that I've been so busy the past couple of weeks. I know December is a tough month for you, and I should have made myself more available."

"Don't worry, the wedding has occupied most of my spare time, so I haven't had much opportunity to sit and stew. I know it's only been two years, but I can't imagine ever truly celebrating on my actual birthday again. Aunt Alice is throwing a little party for me on Saturday instead. I'm sure she'll invite you both."

"And there's a silver lining for you tomorrow, isn't there, Beth?" Natasha grinned.

"Finally. Todd and I will be officially dating on my sweet sixteenth. He's taking me out to dinner and everything."

All three girls squealed and ended up in a group hug.

Someone knocked on the open door, and Sara's mom poked her head around the corner. "Am I interrupting?"

"Mom, no not at all. Come on in."

Natasha and Bethany gathered their belongings and gave Mrs. Dean a quick hug on their way out.

"You look so beautiful, Sara. I can't believe how my little girl is suddenly so mature. You've done a lot of growing up this year, haven't you, dear?"

Sara straightened her mom's pearl necklace. "I guess so. It's been a tough year in some ways, but a fantastic one, too. I'll never forget it." She held her mother's hands in her own. "One of the highlights is our relationship, Mom. It reminds me of how we used to be, years ago."

"Before we lost the little one?" Mrs. Dean's voice was a whisper.

"Yes. It's been a really difficult journey for you, I know that."

"I shut you out and became bitter. I know I've been a nightmare to live with. I don't know how your father has stayed with me all these years."

"Because he loves you, Mom. We all do. Maybe it took the fear of losing another child and then finding him for you to let go of the pain. It opened you up again." Sara held her mom close. "I'm praying for you, Mom."

"I know you are. Don't stop, Sara. My heart is thawing."

A loud knock on the door broke the precious moment. "Five minutes, Miss Dean," someone shouted from the corridor.

"I should go, but first I want to give you this."

Sara took the tiny velvet box from her mother.

"What is it, Mom?"

"It's something I should have given you a long time ago. It was my grandmother's, and then my mother's, and now I think you should have it. I know it will mean something to you."

With that, Mrs. Dean hurried to the door in her high heels, waved at Sara, and disappeared.

Sara flicked open the box, and gasped. It was a small, shiny gold cross, nestled in black satin. She tentatively pulled it out, and it caught the light as it hung suspended on a fine gold chain. With quivering fingers, she threaded the chain under her mass of curls and around her neck. The clasp was tricky, but with the aid of the mirror, the necklace was quickly in place.

"There." Sara took a step back and smiled at her reflection. It wasn't a smug, conceited smile—even though she looked like a million bucks. It was pure joy. She took a few seconds to drink in the blessings.

"Sara Dean, what is going on? Here I am, singing at my concert. How surreal is that? I have the most amazing friends, and a very special wedding coming up in a couple of weeks. Gracelight is giving me the opportunity of a lifetime with my music. James is home, and loving Youth and church. I finally have a beautiful relationship with my mom. I'm learning to give everything to God, including my fears. And now my only worry is that I'm talking to my reflection in the mirror."

She reached up and touched the gold cross. It was so tiny, nobody in the audience would even notice it, but for Sara it was symbolic. Having the cross front and center was important, in her singing and in her life.

Lord, thank you for Your unconditional love. Thank you for being patient with me, for being my loving Heavenly Father. Please help me to keep You front and center. Whatever life throws at me, help me to give my fears over to You. May this concert be for Your glory. I know You hand-picked every person in this audience, including my family and Brittany. Use the words I sing to touch hearts, Lord...

She sang a few more scales, gave her hair one last tussle, and hurried to the side stage. Sara was ready to fearlessly give her everything to the One who gave everything for her.

~ *End* ~

Made in the USA
Charleston, SC
12 December 2015